Freddie,

Happy

11' Tues

James Love

JAMES LOVE

For Mum and Dad

CTRL-ALT-DELETE

'*WAAAAHHHH!*' cried out the two boys in unison as they whirled around and around in a flurry of arms and legs.

'I'm too young to die!' screamed one of the boys, his eyes bulging wide with terror.

'I think I've just wet myself!' exclaimed the other.

The odd shaped spaceship thundered on, punching its way through the Earth's atmosphere and rocketing past the moon, now just a distant grey smudge in its rear viewscreen.

A dim red light flashed intermittently, temporarily illuminating the ship's control room before casting it back into shadow. Like a racing car driver with his pedal to the metal, the immense g-force of the accelerating ship began to pin the two boys back in their chairs, their faces twisting and contorting grotesquely as shockwave after shockwave washed over them.

'Multiverse Drive engaged,' rang out a synthesized female voice. 'Prepare for Quantum jump.'

It sounded strangely calm and tranquil amidst the chaos of the runaway ship, which shuddered and vibrated violently, as if threatening at any moment to tear itself apart.

The two boys struggled to turn their heads, but eventually their eyes met. Speech had become impossible, not that words were needed—their eyes said it all.

How had it come to this?

And then, in a thunderclap of brilliant white light, the ship was gone.

CHAPTER ONE

SCHOOL TRIP BLUES

'Max Voltage?'

'Here, Miss,' replied the small blond-haired boy sat at the front of the bus. He was wedged uncomfortably in his seat, the left side of his face smeared comically against a fogged up window. Next to him was the reason for his discomfort, his best and only friend, Stevie, whose large bottom occupied most of the seat and who was far too absorbed in the packet of crisps he was demolishing to notice his friend's pained expression.

The two boys had been best friends ever since their first day at nursery together, when Stevie had somehow managed to sniff out the naptime biscuits, which he'd promptly gorged himself on. Max never saw the torrent of projectile vomit heading his way, but ever since then the two of them had been inseparable. This, as it turned out, was a good thing, as neither of them were particularly popular with the rest of the class. As if to demonstrate this, a scrunched-up ball of paper flew from the rear of the bus and bounced off the back of Max's head.

Max ignored the laughter behind him and instead sunk lower in his seat. He'd learnt a long time ago to ignore the bullies; they'd soon get bored and move on to their next victim—or so he hoped.

'Watch out you lil' runt!' came a boy's cruel voice. 'Stevie Five Bellies might hoover *you* up as well if you're not careful!'

Stevie momentarily turned his attention from the packet of crisps and replied matter-of-factly over his shoulder, 'I'm not fat. My mum says I'm *metabolically challenged*.'

'Your mum's so fat, she makes Jabba the Hutt look skinny,' shouted back the voice, to a chorus of sniggers from the other children.

'Steven Zimmerman?' interrupted Miss Spittle.

'Er... Miss?'

'Are you here or not, Steven?' she asked, impatiently tapping a bony finger against the side of her clipboard.

Stevie didn't answer. Instead, he shifted uncomfortably in his seat, a growing look of concern on his face. A distant rumble had begun to emanate from deep within his bowels.

And it was getting louder.

PAARRRPPPP! Stevie let off a truly thunderous fart that reverberated loudly against the leather bus seat.

Max pulled his top up over his nose, all too familiar with what was to come.

'Miss! Stinky Stevie's let one rip again, Miss!' called out the precocious, pigtailed girl sat opposite.

'Lucinda, how many times must I tell you, it's *passed wind.* Young ladies do not—OH DEAR LORD!'

Miss Spittle stopped abruptly as the invisible cloud of Stevie's toxic emission assaulted her nostrils like a sledgehammer, and the rest of the bus groaned as the noxious gas travelled slowly down the aisle.

'*S-S-Steven Z-Zimmerman!*' spluttered Miss Spittle. She clutched at her scrawny throat and, through watering eyes, attempted to fix Stevie with a steely glare.

'Better out than in, Miss,' said Stevie unashamedly. 'My mum says it's dangerous not to.'

This was his stock reply after one of his many, frequent, bottom eruptions.

'Maybe if you *ate* less, we wouldn't have this problem, Steven!' exclaimed Miss Spittle, wiping a tear from her cheek.

She turned to the bus driver and leaned down closely to his ear. 'Put your foot down,' she whispered out the corner of her mouth. 'The sooner this day's over, the better!'

The rickety bus of noisy primary school children announced its arrival with a loud backfire from its exhaust, propelling a plume of dirty black smoke high into the air.

'Right then, 6 Alpha,' said Miss Spittle, pausing to pick out a spitball from the back of her rapidly greying hair. 'File out of the bus in an orderly manner. Remember, you're representing the school, so best behaviour at all times.'

She'd barely finished her sentence before the children stampeded past her like a herd of wild buffalo and flew down the steps.

Even though they'd been sat at the front, Max and Stevie were the last to get off. School trips invariably meant more pranks being played on them than normal, and they were in no hurry to leave the relative safety of the bus.

'Come on, boys,' said Miss Spittle, noticing their reluctance. 'You never know, you might even enjoy yourselves.'

And she was right. Not that they were to know it of course, as they grudgingly made their way off the bus, but Max and Stevie were about to embark on the most fantastical adventure of their lives.

The sign on the side of the building read *National Museum of Space Antiquities*.

'That's just another way of saying old space junk,' said Lucinda sarcastically, much to the amusement of the gaggle of giggling girls around her.

'Follow me!' called out Miss Spittle. 'We've a lot to see and not much time to do it in.'

She led the children into the building and past exhibit after exhibit. There were old satellites, old space shuttles, old bits of space rock. You name it, if it was old and had been in space, then it was here.

'*Boorrring!*' said Lucinda, ignoring her surroundings in favour of taking yet another selfie on her phone. In Lucinda's world, the most interesting thing was, well—Lucinda.

Max and Stevie trailed behind the rest of the class, partly to avoid any unwanted attention from the others, and partly to allow Stevie to remain unseen by the prying eyes of Miss Spittle as he devoured yet another packet of crisps. At least, that was the plan.

'Max! Steven! Catch up!' barked Miss Spittle. She peered over the top of her glasses. 'And Steven, don't think I can't see what you're doing.'

'Stevie,' said Max, his voice soft, almost timid. 'We're going to get into trouble.' It was the first time he'd spoken since answering the register back on the bus.

'Hold on, I'm almost finished,' mumbled Stevie through a blizzard of crumbs.

'No, now!' said Max impatiently.

Stevie glanced up from the packet of crisps, a look of surprise on his face. He'd never known his friend, his best friend in the entire universe, to have ever said a cross word to him. Something was definitely up.

'Ah, nice of you to join us,' said Miss Spittle, giving the two boys a withering look as they caught up with the rest of the class. 'Max, maybe you'd like to tell us about this next exhibit.' She pressed a button on the wall, and a huge metal door began groaning in protest as it slowly slid to one side.

The hangar was enormous, perhaps the biggest room Max had ever seen. There, sat in the middle of it, was a massive spaceship that loomed high above the class and made them look like ants in comparison.

'Whoa! That's got to be the biggest rust bucket I've ever seen!' said Lucinda, casting a cynical eye over the ship.

Admittedly, it was a very odd looking craft. Unlike the shiny, sleek spaceships that you see in the movies, its irregular, rusting exterior was a patchwork quilt of mismatched sheets of metal, held in place by thousands of circular rivets that dotted its surface like a bad case of acne. Satellite dishes and strange contraptions sprouted precariously from it, as if randomly stuck on with sticky tape, and a ragged, gaping hole tore through the bottom of its hull.

'Lucinda! Show some respect,' snapped Miss Spittle. 'This ship was the last one designed by Max's father before he… well, before he…'

'Before he went missing,' interjected Max, his voice barely a whisper. 'Presumed dead.'

'You mean your dead dad's responsible for this huge metal monstrosity?' sneered Lucinda contemptuously, an overly dramatic look of disgust on her face.

'Hey, leave off him!' said Stevie, leaping to Max's defence.

'Ooohhh! Touched a nerve have I, Jelly Belly?' asked Lucinda. She was playing to the crowd and enjoying the attention of her little gang of sycophants, who laughed at her every word. 'I'd better be careful,' she continued mockingly. 'I wouldn't want to get on the wrong side of little and large here—odd and odder!'

It was true. Stood side by side, Max and Stevie were a rather strange sight, and an unlikely pairing. Max was skinny and smaller than the average eleven-year-old, with neat blond hair that had clearly been combed by his mum. Stevie, in comparison, was the polar opposite. Large, others less kind may say fat, with a mop of unruly dark hair, which more often than not had the crumbs of his last snack scattered amongst it.

'Hey! Pipsqueak, I'm talking to you.'

But Max was oblivious to Lucinda's hurtful comments. It was his dad's ship alright. There, laser-etched across the side of its huge hull, was the name—*Cosmo II*. Not that he needed proof. He'd seen it briefly once before, in a photo on the wall of his dad's study. It had shown his dad stood proudly in front of the ship, a beaming grin spread from ear to ear. Max had very few memories of his dad, he'd gone missing whilst Max was still a baby, but he did remember that big, broad smile.

More recently though, Max had seen the ship in his dreams. Every night, for the past two months, he'd woken with a start at exactly midnight, his own name still resounding in his ears. It was almost as if the ship was calling him, reminding him it was there, when he'd tried so hard to forget.

'Max? Max, are you alright?' asked Miss Spittle, a concerned look on her face.

Max jolted back to reality.

'I'm sorry, Max; I didn't mean to upset you. Maybe this was a bad idea.'

'It's OK, Miss. Really, I'll be fine.'

'Well, if you're quite sure?'

And so 6 Alpha walked up the metal ramp and disappeared into the dark underbelly of the *Cosmo II*.

CHAPTER TWO

BLAST OFF!

Unfortunately, Lucinda's earlier description of the ship as a 'rust bucket' hadn't been too far from the truth, and the interior of the ship wasn't much better. Bundles of multi-coloured wire hung down from holes in the ceiling, and exposed circuitry pockmarked the metal walls. The lighting constantly flickered, and the automatic sliding doors had jammed, forcing the class to squeeze their way through.

'Oh wow, what a dump!' said Lucinda, addressing her audience.

Stevie threw her an evil glare and gave Max a reassuring pat on the back.

'Still, I suppose it took *some* brains to design this mess. What happened to you, Pipsqueak?'

Max gave a wry smile. According to his mum, his dad had been a mathematical genius who could complete complex formulae and equations involving space and time in his sleep. He, on the other hand, was stuck in the bottom set for maths and could barely do basic algebra. To be honest, he would far rather spend time with Stevie in his darkened bedroom, playing online video games until late into the night. The only bullies there were the ones on the TV screen, and they were quickly despatched by the blast of a disintegrator cannon or the lob of a plasma grenade.

'What can I say?' replied Max, shrugging his shoulders. 'I guess I'm a big disappointment.' He reached out a hand and splayed his fingers against the side of a cold metal wall, as if touching it somehow brought him closer to his dad.

'So come on then, what's the deal with this ship, Pipsqueak?' Like a shark, Lucinda could smell blood in the water and was beginning to circle her victim.

'You know something, you're real nosy,' interrupted Stevie. 'Why don't you leave Max alone and go giggle with your friends somewhere else.'

Lucinda turned up her pointy little nose. 'Come, girls,' she snorted. 'Let's leave these two *losers* to it.' And with that, Lucinda and her little gang disappeared around a corner.

Max and Stevie stood alone in the corridor, the rest of the class vaguely audible in the distance.

'You OK?' asked Stevie.

'I will be,' said Max. 'Thanks.'

'Can I ask you a question?' said Stevie cautiously.

'Sure, anything.'

'What Lucinda said, you know…' Stevie was hesitant. The two boys had no secrets; they told each other everything. But when it came to his dad, Max had always clammed up.

'You want to know about my dad and this ship?' asked Max.

Stevie nodded, almost embarrassed to have asked. However, for once, Max was remarkably forthcoming.

'I don't know much,' said Max. 'Mum talks about it even less than I do. Apparently, dad had been working on some sort of top secret government project; something to do with a new type of space propulsion.'

Stevie looked even more confused than normal. 'Propulsion?'

'Space travel,' explained Max. 'He designed the original *Cosmo*, and the government were so convinced of his success that they asked him to design this ship as well. But something went wrong. One night dad was working late on his own, and he didn't come home. People, men from the military, turned up on the doorstep the next morning. The *Cosmo* had disappeared in *mysterious circumstances*, and dad with it. No trace of anything, or anyone, was left. Almost overnight, the government shut dad's project down, and everything was hushed up. Mum never got any answers to her questions, and after a while, she gave up asking them. The *Cosmo II* became nothing more than an exhibit to be displayed here in the museum.' Max ran a finger along a metallic surface, examining the thick layer of dust that had accumulated on its tip. 'It's been ten years now since he disappeared, but I guess life goes on.'

'Max! Steven! Where are you?' Miss Spittle's voice echoed along the maze of twisting corridors.

'Thanks,' said Stevie.

'For what?'

'You know... for telling me.'

'I guess now's as good a time as any. And if I can't tell a goofball like you, then who can I?' Max gave Stevie a playful jab in his belly. 'Come on, we'd better get moving.'

The class moved from one disappointment to another. Just when it looked like there might be something interesting to see, it would be blocked by a sealed door or a sign which read *Danger, No Entry*—the lurid red lettering only adding to their allure.

Eventually, they made it to the ship's control room, its beating heart where life or death decisions would be made. Surely there would be something interesting to see here? But no, the panels of lights that covered the control consoles remained unlit, the viewscreen blank, the radar silent.

Lucinda lazily flicked a couple of switches back and forth in the hope that something might spark into life.

'Lucinda, stop that at once!' said Miss Spittle. 'Anyhow, you're wasting your time; apart from the lighting, everything here was disconnected a long time ago. Do you really think we'd be allowed on board otherwise?'

'*Pssst!* Max.' whispered Stevie excitedly.

'What is it?'

'Look! Over there!' Stevie pointed to the far side of the control room. There, in the corner, was a bright red vending machine. 'It's Glurg Cola!'

'Glurg what?' asked Max bemused.

'It's only the most delicious cola in the whole wide world! Mum used to give it to me as a baby. They stopped making it years ago, something to do with unforeseen side effects. Never did me any harm.'

Max eyed his rotund friend from head to toe and back again. 'Um, that's not *strictly* true, Stevie.'

'I didn't think I'd ever see a can again. But I guess even a starship captain needs a sugar hit, right?'

Max smiled to himself. It never failed to amaze him how excited Stevie got where food and drink was concerned. 'I hate to break it to you, Stevie, but look around. It's like everything else on this ship; it's turned off.'

Stevie stared disappointedly at the unlit vending machine. Even the plug had been removed.

'Time to go, 6 Alpha,' called out Miss Spittle, herding the children towards the door.

Stevie sighed. 'It's so close, I can almost taste it.'

The class filed out of the control room and through the ship's corridors towards the exit. From their chatter, the children seemed more excited to be leaving than they were when they'd arrived.

Lucinda looked back over her shoulder. 'Hey, Pipsqueak, where's your shadow?'

'Huh?'

'Fatty Bum-Bum. Where is he?'

Max turned around. Stevie was nowhere to be seen. This was highly unusual as he followed Max everywhere, and for him not to be there now, meant something was seriously wrong.

'Stevie!' called out Max. 'Where are you?'

Max had dropped back from the main group and was attempting to retrace his steps. On his own, the flickering lights in the dimly lit corridors were mildly unnerving, and he'd no intention of spending any more time than he had to finding his friend.

'Stevie, stop playing the fool! We need to get back on the bus.'

'Over here!' called out Stevie, panic in his voice. 'I'm in the control room. Hurry!'

Max squeezed himself through the control room doors, unsure of the horror that was about to face him. And it was a horrifying sight alright, but not one which he might have expected. There, crouched down with his large bottom waggling in the air like a distressed duck, was Stevie, his right arm firmly wedged inside the vending machine.

'I should've known,' said Max, bursting into laughter.

'It's not funny, Max! My arm's starting to go numb.'

'Sorry,' said Max, trying to stifle his giggles. 'But you'd be laughing if you could see yourself right now.'

Max stretched his arms as far as he could around Stevie's considerable waist. 'OK... one, two, three, PULL!'

Stevie's arm popped out of the vending machine, closely followed by a can of Glurg Cola. As the two boys fell backwards, they watched, almost in slow motion, as it sailed high above their heads and landed with a *CRASH!* on top of a control console.

'Get off me you great lump!' groaned Max, who was lying squashed beneath Stevie on the floor.

'Oops! Sorry.'

Max walked over to the control console and inspected it for any damage. It looked like they might just have got away with it.

'Phew! That was a close one. For a minute there, I thought we were in *big* trouble.'

'Me too,' said Stevie relieved. 'It'd be a crime to waste a drop.'

Max rolled his eyes and was about to point out the error of Stevie's ways, when the unthinkable happened.

PSHHHHT! Tiny bubbles of cola started to leak from the can. They came out slowly at first, almost teasingly. But then, before either had a chance to react, it began to spray jets of frothing brown cola all over the control panels, which suddenly lit up with dozens of flashing lights.

'ALERT, ALERT!' said a computerized voice. 'Prepare for launch.'

CHAPTER THREE

MEET M.U.M

The black vacuum of space extended as far as the eye could see. Suddenly, in a thunderclap of brilliant white light, the *Cosmo II* appeared from thin air.

Inside the control room Max and Stevie sat in silence, their eyes wide, unblinking.

'Errr... What just happened?' asked Stevie. His hair, which resembled a bird's nest at the best of times, was stood on end as if he'd just seen a ghost.

'Your stomach got us into trouble—*again!*' said Max, rubbing a bruised elbow.

The two boys staggered from their chairs. Max patted himself down, checking for any missing limbs, whilst Stevie hopped around in his trousers, appearing to perform some type of elaborate Irish jig. Pausing for a moment, he let out a huge sigh of relief. Disaster had been averted. They were still dry.

'Help!' called out a faint, muffled voice. 'Help me!'

'You hear that?' asked Max.

'Hear what?'

'Help me someone, please!' came the voice again.

'That!'

Max and Stevie fanned out around the circular control room. The voice was getting louder, the cries more urgent.

'Help me! Oh please help me, someone, anyone!' cried out the voice again. It was interspersed by an unholy, high-pitched wailing, like a wild animal in distress.

'Here!' said Max. 'Behind this door.' He went to reach for the door's access button.

'Wait!' urged Stevie. 'How do we know what's behind there isn't dangerous?'

'Mummy!' sobbed the voice pathetically. 'I want my mummy!'

'Does that answer your question?' said Max, and he pressed the button.

The door slid back to reveal a small

stockroom, its shelves stacked from floor to ceiling with row upon row of cans. Whilst some of them had dislodged during the ship's launch and fallen onto the hard metal floor, others had received a much softer landing. There, sat on the floor, her skirt bunched up around her waist, was a small sobbing girl nursing a dozen lumps and bumps. It was Lucinda.

'Lucinda!' exclaimed Max. 'What are you doing here?'

'I-I followed you,' whimpered Lucinda, 'When you went looking for Smelly Belly.' She gestured dismissively in Stevie's direction. 'You were so busy trying to free him from that vending machine that you didn't notice me behind you.'

'But how on earth did you end up in here?'

'I-I'm not sure. The floor shook; the walls rattled. The next thing I know, I'm swallowed up in here, getting pelted by a hundred cans!' Lucinda burst into tears again, her usual snotty attitude replaced instead by a snotty nose, which ran down her front in long, sticky green ribbons.

'Here,' said Max, offering Lucinda a neatly ironed hankie. His mum never let him leave home without one.

Lucinda snatched it off him and proceeded to blow her nose, making an unnaturally loud noise for such a small girl.

'Oh my!' cried out Stevie, taking a step towards Lucinda. 'I think I'm in love!'

Lucinda recoiled in horror. 'Has Big Bones had a knock on the head or something?'

Stevie continued to move forward. His eyes were like saucers, and the drool that had started to gather in the corner of his mouth was in danger of overflowing. 'You're the most beautiful thing I've ever seen,' he said, stretching out his arms as if to embrace her.

'OK, now I'm *really* starting to freak out,' said Lucinda, slowly and deliberately shuffling back on her bottom.

Just when he looked to be about to sweep her up in his arms, Stevie stepped over Lucinda and up to the shelf behind her.

There was a brief pause, and then Max started to laugh. 'Look!' he said, pointing at the shelves. 'It's not you he wants; it's the cans. It's Glurg Cola!'

Stevie grabbed a can off the shelf and tore feverishly at the ring pull. In one swift movement, he downed the can. Then another, and another. '*Deeee-licious!*' he finally declared, letting out a loud, contented burp.

'Disgusting!' remarked Lucinda, wiping the last tear from her face. 'Now, would someone care to tell me, what in the name of *Simon Cowell* has happened here?'

The three children sat in the control room. During the school trip, it had been dark and silent, but it was now a hive of activity. The walls were covered in panels of different coloured lights which blinked erratically. The radar swirled and *pinged*, and the viewscreen that had previously been blank, now showed the vast swathe of black that was space.

Stevie sat down in a swivel chair. '*Weeeeeehhh!*' he called out gleefully as he spun around and around. He was apparently unconcerned about the seriousness of the situation they'd found themselves in.

'Stevie, will you stop that?' said Max. 'We need to figure out what's happened here.'

'Too right we do,' said Lucinda, who had by now regained her composure and reverted to her usual, objectionable self. 'Maybe Miss Spitalot and the others are still on board and can shed some light on this mess?'

'Negative, young miss,' interrupted an unseen, matronly voice. It had an artificial quality to it, as if it wasn't quite real. 'I detect no other life forms on board.'

Like meerkats on sentry duty, Stevie and Lucinda swivelled their heads around the room, trying to identify where the voice had come from. Max, however, was still. He'd heard that voice before; it was the voice that had announced the ship's launch. It was the ship's computer.

'Of course!' proclaimed Max to the others. 'This ship, it's fitted with a voice recognition interface system.'

'Plain English please,' sniped Lucinda.

'Mum told me that dad fitted this ship with a uniquely intelligent computer. Rather than typing in commands, it responds to your voice. Tell it what to do, and it'll do it.'

'That is correct, young master,' stated the

computer. 'I am the ship's Multi Universe Matrix, or M.U.M for short.'

'OK, *M.U.M*,' said Lucinda dubiously. 'If you're such a know it all, then tell us what's happened here. Where are we?'

'The Multiverse Drive was engaged, young miss. According to my data banks, the jump was successful.'

'What do you mean *jump*?' asked Max. 'And who activated the Multi...thingy, whatchamacallit?'

'I did, young master,' replied M.U.M. I have transported us from your known universe to the one that we are currently occupying.'

Max looked puzzled. 'Whoa, slow down. How is any of this possible?'

'Your father calculated the existence of multiple universes, some much like home, some very alien to you. He created a propulsion system to enable this ship to access them—the Multiverse Drive.'

'I knew he was working on something top secret, but this? You mean we're no longer in *our* universe?' asked Max incredulously.

'That is correct, young master.'

'Hold on just one minute,' interrupted Lucinda. 'You still haven't answered my question. If we're no longer in our own universe, then exactly what universe *are* we in?'

'Alas, young miss, that is a question to which I do not have the answer.'

'So, not so smart after all, eh?' said Lucinda. 'And here I was thinking you're supposed to be some kind of whizzy-whizz supercomputer.'

'Indeed, young miss. Ordinarily, I would be able to *plug in* to any given universe and instantly download all data regarding it. Unfortunately, some of my circuits were damaged during launch by an unidentified viscous liquid.'

Max threw Stevie a knowing look. Glurg Cola had a lot to answer for.

'Great, just great,' said Lucinda. 'So we're stuck who knows where in this pathetic excuse for a spaceship, and all we have to help us is some jumped up *Alexa* wannabe with a screw loose. Brilliant. Next, you'll be telling me there's no Wi-Fi here either. There is Wi-Fi, right?' She looked down at her phone, her face contorting in despair. '*NOOOOOO!*'

'You said *you* activated the Multiverse Drive,'

continued Max. 'Why?'

'It was necessary to facilitate the rescue of your father, young master.'

'WHAT!' exclaimed Max, sitting bolt upright in his chair. 'My dad's alive? How do you know?'

'My matrix incorporates a cybernetic interface.'

'Meaning what?'

'Your father designed and created me using cells extracted from his own brain tissue. As a result, I have a cybernetic link with your father and any of his descendants, a type of telepathy if you will. Were you not aware of me trying to contact you, young master?'

Max thought for a second. Suddenly, it all became clear.

'The dreams I've been having, you're responsible for them, aren't you? But why now, after all this time?'

'That is correct. Only now are you old enough for me to safely attempt a telepathic link. It was not my intention to alarm you, but you are needed if we are to successfully retrieve your father. It was indeed fortuitous that your school trip brought us together.'

'But if you knew my dad was still alive, why wait to tell me? What about the government, the men from the military? Surely you told them?'

'Indeed I did, young master. Unfortunately, they ignored what I had to say and instead ordered that my circuits be immediately severed in the interests of national security. However, as you are now aware, I still function.'

'So let me get this right,' said Lucinda. 'You're like, *alive?*'

'In a sense, young miss, yes.'

Lucinda turned to Max. 'Ha! So M.U.M's also your dad. Talk about confusing.'

'Professor Voltage is a great man, young miss. It was natural that he combine his superior intellect with my own.'

'So where is he? *Where's* dad?' asked Max, impatiently pacing around the control room. 'What are we doing wasting our time here? We should be looking for him.'

'My proximity sensors have not been activated, young master. It has not been possible to establish a link with your father. Whilst I am aware of his continued existence, I am not, however, able to pinpoint his location.'

'Then try harder!' urged Max.

'A link can only be achieved when we both occupy the same space and time. As this has not been possible, the only logical conclusion is that your father does not exist in this current universe.'

'So do another jump, to a universe where he does. Please, we must find him.'

'Regretfully, it is not that simple, young master. Your father disappeared before he was able to perfect the Multiverse Drive's navigational system. Whilst it is possible to jump to another universe, there is no way of guaranteeing which one it will be.'

'Then there's no time to waste. Do it, fire up the Multiverse Drive!'

'Negative, young master. The ship's Multiverse Drive has been damaged by the same viscous liquid that has corrupted my matrix.'

Max glowered at Stevie. 'If we weren't best friends I'd...'

'ALERT! ALERT!' rang out M.U.M. 'METEOR SHOWER!'

A tremor shook the ship, accompanied by a faint rattle like hailstones on a tin roof.

Quickly, the rattle became a roar as meteors the size of footballs battered the exterior of the ship, which shook and shuddered with every impact.

'FIRE!' screamed Lucinda.

A control console had exploded in a shower of sparks, and flames were starting to lick at the air.

'M.U.M, do something!' shouted Max urgently.

'Behind you, young master.'

Max turned around, steadying himself as the ship continued to shake. Against a wall stood a tall glass cabinet. The glass was frosted, obscuring what was inside, but the large red letters stencilled over it couldn't have been clearer—*In Case of Emergency Break Glass*.

'Do it!' shouted Stevie. 'The flames are getting higher!'

Max grabbed at a hammer that hung from the cabinet by a chain. He hesitated for a second and then, through half shut eyes, smashed the glass, shattering it into a million pieces. Almost instantly, a metal ramp slammed to the floor, and Max was forced to jump out the way as a robot on tank tracks rolled down it. Its eyes, which appeared to be made from old motorcycle headlamps, flashed a bright yellow, and its coiled metal arms waved around wildly.

'What is the nature of the emergency?' queried the robot. It was remarkably well spoken and reminded Max of the butler from his mum's favourite TV show, *Posh Snobs and Paupers*.

'FIRE!' screamed the children, pointing at the flames.

The robot rolled over to the burning console and opened a door in its chest. Reaching in, it whipped out a fire extinguisher and promptly smothered the flames under a billowing white cloud of carbon dioxide gas.

'Who'd have thought it, saved by a talking shopping trolley,' said Lucinda, managing to stand upright as the meteor shower finally passed.

'Ignore her,' said Max, flapping his arms to waft away the remnants of smoke. 'What she means to say is *thank you*.'

'I am the ship's emergency droid, twenty first generation series, sir,' said the robot. 'You may call me ED-21. I am happy to have been of service... Happy... so happy, I could cry... Sad, so sad...'

ED-21 started to spin around wildly on his tracks, silver sparks flying from his head. Suddenly, he slumped forward and fell silent, the light behind his eyes flickering before going out completely.

'What was that all about?' asked Stevie, examining ED-21's gently smouldering head.

'Do not be alarmed, young master. Professor Voltage fitted the emergency droid with an emotion chip in order to act more human. It has confused his circuits and forced a temporary shutdown. He will resume normal functioning shortly.'

'Oh this just gets better by the minute,' said Lucinda. 'As if things weren't bad enough, we've now got this heap of junk to deal with as well.'

'Well that *heap of junk* just saved our lives, so why don't you try being nice for just once in your life,' said Max, finally losing his patience with Lucinda's constant jibes.

'Ooh, look who's found his voice. What's the matter, Pipsqueak? Getting a bit tetchy, are we? I think someone needs a nap.'

'I think we all do,' interrupted Stevie, stretching his arms wide and yawning. 'Although something to eat first would be nice, I'm *starving.*'

Max smiled, the tension broken. It had been a long day, and ED-21 wasn't the only one getting overly emotional. Getting out of bed that morning, he could barely have dreamt he would end the day in another universe, let alone find out that his long-lost dad was still alive.

'Crew living quarters are located on deck five, young master.'

'Come on,' said Max, beckoning to the other two. 'Tomorrow's another day, and something tells me that things are going to get *pretty* exciting around here.'

CHAPTER FOUR

QUAD BIKES AND CAKE

Max opened his eyes. He hadn't slept that well in a long time. For a moment, he forgot where he was, as if at any minute he expected his mum to call him down for breakfast. And then the incredible events of the previous day came flooding back, forcing him to stir and sit up in the metal bunk bed in which he'd slept. Above him, Stevie snored loudly.

M.U.M had directed the three children to the crew living quarters the night before, at least it might have been night, it's pretty hard to tell when you're in space. The boys had taken the first room in a corridor that stretched as far as the eye could see, Stevie calling dibs on the top bunk. Lucinda, meanwhile, had insisted that girls needed their privacy and had taken the room next door. That, and the fact she would rather have fired herself out of one of the ship's airlocks than have to share a room with two smelly boys.

PAARRRPPPP! Stevie announced he was awake with a loud fart.

Max punched the mattress above him, and Stevie let out a yelp.

'Breakfast time!' said Stevie enthusiastically. He threw himself down from the top bunk, and Max suddenly found himself confronted by Stevie's large, wobbling bottom, just centimetres from his face.

'Yikes! I know we're in space, Stevie, but there's only one moon I want to see!'

'Oops! Sorry,' said Stevie, pulling up his moth-eaten underpants.

He walked over to the food dispenser, a small metal hatch in the wall, and pressed a green button. A nozzle dispensed a disgusting looking grey gruel, making a rather unappealing sound—not unlike the one Stevie had just made. He then walked over to a metal table and sat down on a metal chair. In fact, pretty much everything in the room was made of metal and was the same uninspiring shade of metallic grey.

'Eurgh! How can you eat that?' asked Max, grimacing as Stevie enthusiastically shovelled the 'food' into his mouth with a spoon. He'd tried eating it the night before, but had given up in favour of a half-eaten chocolate bar that had been slowly melting in his anorak pocket. It had tasted OK, once he'd picked the fluff off it.

'You know, it's really not that bad once you get used to it,' said Stevie, wiping his chin on the back of his hand. 'And who knows how long we're going to be stuck out here.'

Max got out of bed and walked over to a small circular window that was set into the metal wall like a sailing ship's porthole. As his eyes slowly adjusted, tiny pinpricks of light began to appear, stars that were hundreds, maybe even thousands of light years away. His dad was out there, somewhere. He might not be in this universe, but he was in one of them, and Max was going to do whatever it took to find him.

Just as his mind began to wander, the faint but unmistakable sound of music began to drift into the room from next door. It sounded like one of those annoying boy bands the girls at school swooned over, all sticky up hair and shiny white teeth.

'Isn't that Boys'R Us?' asked Stevie.

'I think it is, but how?' said Max. 'It's too loud to be coming from her phone.'

The two boys hurriedly got dressed and went out into the corridor. The music was louder now, and it was definitely coming from Lucinda's room. Intrigued, Max pressed the buzzer on her door.

'You may enter,' said a regal sounding voice.

The door slid back to reveal an Aladdin's Cave of treasures, and a particularly smug looking Lucinda. 'Ah, welcome to my boudoir, *losers*,' she said haughtily, her right arm swooping in a grand gesture of welcome. She was reclined on a four-poster bed, surrounded by a small mountain of colourful silk pillows and plush cushions. The music Max had heard in his room was indeed coming from her phone. However, it was attached to a fancy looking docking station with two, state-of-the-art, stereo speakers sat either side of it. In fact, the whole room couldn't have been more different to the boys' own, decked out as it was with all the latest gadgets and luxuries that you could imagine. Even its walls had been covered in flowery wallpaper, and posters of the same preening boy band that blared from the speakers were plastered all over them.

ED-21 came zooming into the room on his tracks, a frilly white apron tied around his waist. 'Ah, sirs, just in time for breakfast.' The light in his headlamp eyes began to swirl around and around. A bell *dinged,* and he opened the same door in his chest from which he'd pulled out the fire extinguisher the night before. Only this time he pulled out a tray, upon which teetered a towering stack of steaming hot pancakes.

'What the?' said Max amazed.

Stevie barrelled past him and towards the pancakes. If it was a choice between an explanation or food, his stomach won every time.

'I suppose you're wondering what's going on?' asked Lucinda, admiring her newly manicured nails.

'Er... yeah, you could say that,' replied Max.

'I couldn't sleep last night, so I took a walk around the ship. I made it to the control room, when who should I bump into but dear old ED-21 here. Turns out he's quite a handy robot to have around.' She beckoned him over with a click of her fingers. 'ED-21, make me a chocolate cake.'

'Of course, madam.' His eyes swirled for a couple of seconds, then *ding!* he pulled out a perfectly made chocolate cake from his chest.

'Chocolate cake! Gimme!' cried out Stevie, as if the grey gruel and pancakes had barely touched his sides.

'I am programmed with over a million different recipes and proficient in a number of different culinary styles, sir,' said ED-21.

'And it doesn't stop with recipes,' said Lucinda. 'Check this out. ED-21, make me a dining table.'

Again, his eyes swirled for a moment, and he then began to pull long planks of wood from out of his chest. Max wasn't quite sure how, as they were far too big to be able to fit inside. It was similar to a magic show his mum had taken him to once, where the magician had pulled out all manner of unfeasibly large objects from just a small black bag.

'Pretty amazing, huh?' said Lucinda, as ED-21 set about hammering in nails in super-quick time. 'He can even sort you and Big Boy out with some new clothes.' She looked Max up and down disdainfully. 'Not exactly *designer,* are we?'

'ED-21 is an emergency droid, Lucinda,' said

Max, self-consciously threading a finger through a hole in his top. 'Not your own personal slave to order around.'

'Um… Max,' interrupted Stevie, spraying a mouthful of cake crumbs into the air. 'You might want to try a slice of this first, especially as you don't like the ship's food.'

Max eyed the chocolate cake suspiciously. There was no denying, it certainly looked good. Surely there was no harm in having just *one* bite? Except Max had several, and before he knew it, he'd eaten the whole slice, the only proof it had ever existed the small smudge of chocolate icing smeared across his top lip. 'Yes, well, I suppose I could make an exception, just this once you understand,' he said sheepishly.

ED-21 beckoned the three children to take a seat around the newly made dining table. Once Max got used to the idea, it was soon straining under the weight of a small mountain of bacon sandwiches, which the children hungrily wolfed down.

'I am sorry to disturb you, young master,' rang out M.U.M's voice from the heavens, 'but I have a progress report for you.'

'That's OK, M.U.M, go ahead,' said Max, wiping his mouth on a paper napkin.

'I have good news and bad news. The good news is that the repairs to my corrupted matrix are almost complete. An information download regarding this universe is imminent.'

'That's great,' said Max. 'And the bad?'

'It would appear that the damage to the ship's Multiverse Drive is greater than I had first feared.'

Stevie screwed up his face and mouthed 'Sorry' to Max.

'It will also be necessary to replenish its power source.'

'Power source?' asked Max.

'Specifically, a rare mineral called Multinium. It can only be found in certain types of asteroid.'

'You mean like space rocks?'

'That is a rather simplistic way of putting it, young master, but yes. Your father fitted this ship with a laser drill for the purpose of mining asteroids and accessing the Multinium within them.'

'OK, so what happens next?'

'I am running a scan for a suitable asteroid

as we speak. I will inform you as soon as I have located one.'

'There you go then,' said Stevie, looking up from the chocolate cake. Almost his entire face was hidden under a mask of brown icing, so that only the whites of his eyes were visible. 'Until then, I say we kick back and get ED-21 to cook us up some more tasty treats.'

'I concur with young Master Stevie,' said M.U.M. 'I do not detect any nearby planetary systems, and it may be some time before my scan is successful. May I suggest that you all rest and take in the appropriate nourishment?'

'Rest?' said Lucinda. 'But we've only just got up.'

'Yes, young miss, but you will require all your energy for the challenges ahead.'

'*Challenges*? What challenges? Look, I've had just about enough of this nonsense…'

'Food and rest it is then,' interrupted Max. He gave Lucinda the sternest look he could muster, which admittedly wasn't very stern at all. 'Don't worry, M.U.M, I'll make sure of it.'

'YEE-HA!' shouted Stevie, as he roared down a corridor on a bright red quad bike. 'Race ya!'

Max followed some distance behind, taking a rather more cautious approach. His intentions had been good at first; after all, he'd given M.U.M his word that they'd all rest. But staying in your room at home is one thing. Staying in your room when it's part of a massive spaceship travelling through the deep space of a parallel universe, is a completely different matter altogether. Add to that ED-21's ability to create almost anything, with the wild imaginations of two young boys, and you had a potentially explosive combination.

Their requests had been small at first. New clothes were a necessity. They didn't want to be smelly, or in Stevie's case *smellier*. But as they gazed in wonder at ED-21's 'box of tricks', their imaginations had begun to take over. Large, comfortable beds would make sleeping more pleasant. A games console would help to pass the time. And quad bikes? Well, they would be FUN!

The two boys whizzed along the rabbit warren of corridors, marvelling at just how big the ship was. Big, and boring. Most rooms were full of antiquated machinery that wheezed and whined, and occasionally a jet of steam would escape from the maze of metal piping that zigzagged high above their heads. Huge cabinets with wildly spinning spools of computer tape inside them lined the walls, whilst others spat out long reams of perforated paper that coiled snake-like onto the floor. Cutting edge technology this most definitely wasn't, and instead everything on the ship appeared to have been salvaged from a scrapyard or found in the dusty backroom of a charity shop. In fact, it was such a mishmash of obsolete equipment that Max wondered how the ship had ever made it off the ground in the first place. His dad really *must* be a genius.

Max accelerated up alongside Stevie. 'You know, maybe we should go back and check on Lucinda,' he shouted over the growl of the quad bikes' engines. As much as he disliked her, Max felt bad about leaving Lucinda on her own.

'Lucinda?' shouted back Stevie. 'Lucinda, who puts us down at every opportunity and calls us nasty names? *That* Lucinda? What do we care?'

'Look, I'm no fan of hers either, Stevie, but she's... you know, a girl, and girls are more...' He struggled to find the word. 'Sensitive.'

'Sensitive!' exclaimed Stevie. 'Lucinda's about as sensitive as a bull in a china shop. And anyhow, she's the one that decided to stay sulking in her room.'

'*Stevie,*' said Max.

Stevie recognised that tone of voice. It was the same one his mum used to 'guilt trip' him into kissing his ancient Aunt Beryl on the lips when she came to visit, even though she smelled funny and had a big hairy wart on her chin that tickled his neck.

'You know, if she hadn't been snooping on us in the first place then she wouldn't even be here…'

'*Stevie.*'

'Fine, have it your way,' said Stevie reluctantly. 'But don't say I didn't warn you.'

'What do you want?' snapped Lucinda. She was lying on her front on the four-poster bed, her chin slumped in her hands. It was plain for all to see that she was throwing a massive sulk, and she wanted *everyone* to know about it.

'Stevie and I were wondering if you wanted a game of *Zombie Death Kill* on the games console?' said Max tentatively. 'I'm sure we could get ED-21 to sort us out with a third controller.'

'You just don't get it, do you?' sneered Lucinda.

'Get what?' asked Max.

'Hmm... well let me see,' she replied sarcastically. 'For starters, there's no phone service here, wherever *here* is. There's no Instagram, no Snapchat—no nothing. I'm a social outcast, and it's all your fault. You and Fat Boy there.' She jabbed a finger in Stevie's direction. 'If I want to hang out with the two biggest losers in school, then I'll let you know. Now get out of my room and leave me alone!' She picked up a cushion and threw it at Max who dodged out the way, only for it to hit Stevie full in the face instead.

'Ow! That hurt,' said Stevie, rubbing his nose.

'You know, you might not like us very much, Lucinda,' said Max. 'But guess what? We're not too keen on you either. I just thought we could all try to get along, that's all.'

He looked at Stevie who was still clutching his nose. 'You were right, there's no point talking to her.'

'Whatever!' shouted Lucinda, as the two boys turned their backs on her and walked out the room, the doors sliding closed behind them.

CHAPTER FIVE

A LOT OF SNOT

The zombie lurched forward. '*Brains,*' it groaned, licking its purple lips with what was left of its rotten tongue. A juicy fat maggot wriggled out of an empty eye socket and fell to the floor.

'Max, help me! I'm surrounded!' shouted Stevie.

Max somersaulted through the air, nimbly landing on his feet. In the same movement, he released his catapult and a marble flew through the air, hitting the lead zombie squarely between the eyes with a satisfying *THUD!* It let out a low, guttural moan and then toppled over face first.

'Max, hurry!'

'I'm almost there, Stevie. Hold on!'

Max ducked under a decomposing arm, avoiding the long, razor-sharp nails that slashed at his face. He fired another marble, and another zombie was consigned to hell.

'Just two more left, Max. You can do it!'

'But I've only got one marble left though!'

'Then think of something, and make it quick or I'm going to end up as the filling in a zombie sandwich!'

Max skilfully sidestepped one zombie and body swerved the next. He was waiting, carefully choosing his moment… *SNAP!* The catapult propelled the marble through the air with expert precision, hitting the head of the first zombie before ricocheting off at an angle and impacting the forehead of the second with a loud *CRACK!* Their bodies slumped to the floor, twitched for a moment, then fell still.

'Yes!' said Stevie, punching the air. 'I knew you could do it.'

'Pretty nifty shooting there, Pipsqueak,' came Lucinda's voice from behind them. Max and Stevie had been so engrossed in their video game that her entrance had gone unnoticed.

'What do you expect?' asked Stevie, taking off his virtual reality headset. 'He's *DeadlyAssassin11*, no one can beat him.'

Max threw Stevie a sideways glance, which was code for 'Shut up'.

'You're *DeadlyAssassin11*? The champion of online gaming? No way, I don't believe it. He's like, a legend at school,' said Lucinda sceptically.

'Believe it,' said Stevie. 'You saw him in action. No one else could have pulled off that move.'

Max threw Stevie another glance, only this time his eyes were bulging, and a little blue vein in his temple had started to throb rhythmically.

'What?' asked Stevie. 'Max, we're in space, who knows where. Letting Lucinda into our little secret isn't going to change anything.'

'No way,' said Lucinda. 'You really are *DeadlyAssassin11*. What's with all the secrecy, Pipsqueak? The kids at school might've gone a bit easier on you if they'd known.'

'I didn't want to draw attention to myself,' replied Max, before quickly changing the subject. 'Anyhow, why are you even here, I thought we weren't good enough to be in your company?'

'Yes, well. I've been thinking about what you said, you know, about us all getting along. I suppose I could bring myself to be in your company, just for a bit you understand. Until we find a way home.'

'How good of you,' said Max, giving Lucinda a taste of her own sarcasm.

'Errr… I hate to interrupt, but can anyone else see what I can?' asked Stevie, pointing towards the small circular window.

Outside, looking in, was what appeared to be a small green slug-like creature. Two stalks with bulging eyeballs on either end protruded from what might have been its head, but could just as easily have been its bottom. It was hard to tell.

'OMG! It's an alien!' screamed Lucinda, flapping her arms in panic.

Her response seemed to startle the creature, which crawled off the window and out of sight, leaving behind a luminous green trail of slime.

'M.U.M, are you there?' asked Max.

'Affirmative, young master. I am scanning the life form. Processing… Please wait.'

Two blinking eyeballs on the end of stalks reappeared at the window. On seeing there was no immediate danger, the creature's body followed closely behind, making a sound like a squeegee as it smeared itself across the glass.

'Processing complete,' said M.U.M. 'A genetic scan indicates that the life form currently staring in the window is closely related to—young Master Stevie.'

'Eh?' said Stevie, dumbfounded.

'Stevie, what have you done this time?' asked Max.

'Nothing, honest!'

'To be more specific, it would appear that the life form has evolved from young Master Stevie's mucous secretions,' said M.U.M.

'Does she always have to speak like that?' asked Lucinda. 'How about in a language we can all understand?'

'I think I get it,' said Max. 'What she means to say is that slug, alien, whatever you want to call it, has evolved from Stevie's snot. Am I correct, M.U.M?'

'Indeed you are, young master. It would appear that a sample of young Master Stevie's nasal discharge somehow found its way onto the exterior of the ship. I can only conclude that the radiation, unleashed by the ship when the Multiverse Drive was activated, did in some way alter the bacteria present in his, as you say, snot. An evolutionary process that would normally have taken millions of years has been rapidly accelerated, and this life form is the end result.'

'Ew! Gross!' said Lucinda. 'Congratulations Belly Boy, you're a dad.'

'Anything you want to add to that, Stevie?' asked Max.

'Ummm… I… Errr… 'There is *one* thing I can think of that, maybe, just maybe, might have happened.'

'Go on,' said Max, 'We're listening.'

'You remember that bag of crisps I was eating, the ones you wouldn't let me finish?'

'Yeah, what about them?'

'Well, you were still in a bit of a daze when we walked up the ramp into the ship, so I took the opportunity to quickly snaffle what was left of them. Trouble is, they were beef and pepper flavour and…' Stevie's mind began to wander as he recollected the delicious taste of the crisps. His eyes had gone all dreamy, and he licked his lips as if he could still taste them.

'Stevie! Stop thinking about the crisps and get on with the story.'

'Oh, yeah, sorry. Well, some of the pepper went up my nose, making me want to sneeze. I

didn't have a tissue, which wouldn't normally
be too much of a problem. But when you're still
getting over a cold, it makes things a bit more…
gooey.'

Lucinda dry heaved. 'Someone get me a
bucket, I think I'm gonna vom!'

'*Shhh!* Let him finish,' said Max.

'I had no choice but to sneeze into my hand
and then I… I….' Stevie hesitated for a moment,
embarrassed to admit what he'd done.

'And then you what?' prompted Max, although
he was pretty sure that he already knew the
answer. Whilst most people were generally
repelled by Stevie's unnatural bodily functions,
Max had become oblivious to them long ago.
Still, it amused him to see the look of horror on
other people's faces. And right now, Lucinda's
was a picture.

'And then I wiped my hand down the outside
of the ship,' blurted out Stevie, relieved to have
finished his confession.

'You know, you really *are* disgusting,' said
Lucinda through her fingers.

'Look, we can talk about Stevie's manners, or
lack of them, later,' said Max. 'But right now, we

need to decide what to do with that thing outside the window.'

'Well I say we leave it out there,' said Lucinda. 'It's creeping me out.'

'We can't do that. It's a living creature,' said Stevie.

'Agreed,' said Max. 'It's not right to just leave it out there. M.U.M, what do you think?'

'The life form does not appear to be dangerous, young master. I can beam it inside using the ship's teleportation device.'

'Do it,' said Max, before Lucinda was able to object.

The three children stared out of the window and watched in fascination as the strange slug creature disappeared in a sparkling golden haze.

'*Bleurgh!*' came a noise from behind them. The three children whirled around and were confronted by the sight of the creature looking back at them. Before they had a chance to react, it charged at them and sent them scattering. All except Lucinda, who stood transfixed to the spot as the creature jumped up into her arms. Just when she thought it was about to bite her head off, it shot out a long slimy tongue and licked her face affectionately.

'Aww, look. It likes her,' said Stevie.

'GET IT OFF! GET IT OFF, GET IT OFF!' screamed Lucinda, slime dripping down her face.

'*Bleurgh! Bleurgh!*' yipped the odd creature, snuggling into the curve of Lucinda's neck. It was like an excited puppy trying to bark, but the noise that came out sounded more like a chronic asthmatic with a heavy cold.

'Snot, here boy,' called out Stevie.

The creature jumped out of Lucinda's arms and 'ran' over to Stevie, tenderly rubbing its head against his ankles. Of course, it didn't run in the conventional sense; after all, it had no legs. Instead, it used its slimy tail to perform a type of superfast wiggle that propelled it along at a rate of knots.

'Snot?' asked Max.

'Well, he's got to have a name,' said Stevie.

'He? How can you tell?'

'I can't, I just know.' Stevie bent down and stroked Snot's head, coating his palm in mucous. 'You know, he's quite cute really.'

'CUTE!' roared Lucinda. 'CUTE! Have you seen what that thing's done to me?'

Lucinda was quite a sight. From her waist up, she was covered in a thick layer of green goo that dripped down in long treacle-like strands onto the floor.

'I think that look suits you,' joked Stevie. 'Really brings out your eyes.' He looked at Max, and the two boys collapsed in a fit of laughter.

'Urgh! I'm having a shower!' said Lucinda, and she stormed out the room, leaving a trail of slime in her wake.

'Looks like we've got a new addition to the crew,' said Max, and the two boys burst out laughing again.

CHAPTER SIX

CAPTAIN MAX

'Help!' called out Stevie.

Max ran to the bathroom door and put his ear up against it. 'Stevie, you OK? I'm coming in.'

'No, wait!' called out Stevie, but it was too late.

Max pressed the access button and the door slid across. There, floating around the room was Stevie, naked apart from a small towel to cover his modesty.

'M.U.M, what's going on?' asked Max.

'A temporary gravity failure has occurred in the bathroom area, young master. I am attempting to fix it.'

Lucinda appeared at the door alongside Max, closely followed by Snot who, despite her protests, had clearly taken a liking to her. 'Does nothing in this ship work properly?' she asked, grimacing at the sight before her. She was about to launch into another of her diva-ish rants, when her attention was caught by the curious looking object slowly orbiting around Stevie. 'Um, what's that thing floating next to Chubba Bubba?'

'What thing?' asked Max, following her gaze. And then his jaw dropped. 'Oh no, it's not? Stevie, tell me that's not what I think it is.'

'I couldn't help it!' cried out Stevie, bouncing off the ceiling. 'I was doing my business when the gravity failed. It's not my fault!'

'You don't mean to say that thing floating around is… is his…' Lucinda couldn't bring herself to say it.

'His poo,' said Max. 'Yep, that's Stevie's poo.'

Before the horror of the situation had a chance to fully sink in, Snot suddenly shot out his long lizard-like tongue and expertly lassoed the poo, dragging it back into his mouth before swallowing it with an almighty *GULP!* As Stevie so often did after a good meal, Snot copied his master and let out an extremely loud, satisfied burp, his mouth quivering with its ferocity.

'Ew! Poo breath! I can almost taste it!' exclaimed Lucinda, gasping for breath. 'That has to be the most disgusting thing I've ever seen!'

At that exact moment the gravity switched back on, and Stevie fell to the floor in a heap, minus his towel, which drifted gently to the floor a couple of seconds later.

'Ewww! Correction—second most disgusting thing!'

'Attention,' said M.U.M, her voice more urgent than normal. 'I have detected several ships heading our way. Please convene in the control room.'

'We're on our way, M.U.M,' replied Max. He looked down at Stevie who was desperately scrabbling about on the floor in an attempt to cover himself up. 'You might want to put some clothes on first though,' he said with a chuckle.

The control room doors slid open, and in walked the three children, Snot yipping at their feet. Lucinda flicked him away with the toe of her shoe, only to look down in despair at the slimy green residue that had been left behind on it.

'I am activating the viewscreen now, young master,' said M.U.M.

The viewscreen lit up with a grey fuzz before clearing to reveal the blackness of space. At first glance, it looked as if there was nothing else to see, but then, in the distance, the three children could just make out a small rust-coloured spaceship. Two, slightly larger, shiny silver spaceships were chasing it and were spitting out purple laser beams that scythed in its direction.

Max squinted at the view screen. 'It's so far away; can't we get a better look?'

'Magnify,' said M.U.M.

The viewscreen automatically zoomed in on the unfolding action. It soon became clear that the smaller of the ships wasn't rust-coloured at all. It *was* rust. Desperately, it zigzagged back and forth in a vain attempt to avoid the barrage of laser fire from the other two ships.

'That hardly seems fair,' said Stevie. 'Two against one; we should help them.'

'It's not our fight, Stevie,' said Max. 'Who knows what we'd be getting involved in.' He turned his back to the viewscreen, as if ignoring it would make it go away.

'Typical Pipsqueak,' remarked Lucinda. 'Anything for a quiet life.'

A purple laser beam sliced through one of the smaller ship's two engines, clinically shearing it off like a surgeon amputates a limb. But still it continued to flee, its one remaining engine burning brightly in a valiant attempt to propel the ship to safety.

'Max! We can't just leave them,' pleaded Stevie.

'My sensors indicate that the alien ship's life support systems will fail if we do not intervene now, young master.'

'So what's it going to be, Pipsqueak? You can't hide away your whole life you know.'

'Ninety seconds until critical, young master.'

'Fine, OK!' snapped Max. 'But who made me captain?'

He looked at Stevie and Lucinda to put themselves forward, but neither of them did, for two very different reasons. Stevie was, well, Stevie, and as big a heart as he had, when it came to responsibility, it was fair to say he couldn't be relied upon. Give him a goldfish to look after, and it would be belly up in the water the next day. Lucinda, on the other hand, was all mouth. Behind her acid tongue and abrasive personality was a frightened little girl who was afraid of being on her own, although she would rather die than admit it.

'That's just great; me it is then,' said Max, who on the face of it was perhaps the unlikeliest of the three to take command. What Lucinda had said before was true; he *had* hidden away his whole life. Ever since his dad had disappeared, his mum had wrapped him up in cotton wool, afraid to let him out of her sight. Whilst the other children had played outside, Max had remained cocooned in his bedroom playing video games, his only contact with the outside world Stevie, and the faceless voices that drifted down his gaming headset. That was fine by him, but as the seasons had changed outside his window, he'd retreated more and more into their artificial worlds. The 'real' world had become alien to him, making him an easy target for the playground bullies who would taunt and call him names. Of course, Stevie did his best to stick up for him, but then he had issues of his own to deal with. More often than not, Max would ignore them, zip up the fur-lined hood of his anorak tightly around his face, and walk on.

Unfortunately, zipping up his hood now wasn't an option. Whether he liked it or not, it was up to Max to take the lead.

'M.U.M, what weapons do we have?'

'Your father did not fit this ship with conventional weapons. However, the ship's laser drill can be utilised for that purpose, should you so wish.'

'Er… I guess so,' said Max hesitantly. His manner wasn't exactly inspiring confidence in the others.

'Very well. Take a seat, young master. I will transfer control of the laser drill to you now.'

Max sat down in the captain's chair, which dwarfed his tiny frame and left his feet dangling in the air. A joystick, clearly made for much bigger hands, automatically popped out of the armrest.

'Stevie, if we're going to have any chance of doing this, then I'm going to need you to work the radar console.'

'Sixty seconds until critical. You must act now, young master.'

'Stevie, how far away are the ships?'

Stevie stared gormlessly at the radar screen. 'Um… well, let me see. The pinging sound is getting faster, if that means anything? Oh, and look, the two big flashing lights are getting closer to the smaller one.'

'Useless,' said Lucinda, rolling her eyes. She leaned across Stevie and scrutinised the display. 'Two kilometres and closing, Pipsqueak.'

Max tentatively took hold of the joystick, and a red targeting sight instantly appeared on the viewscreen. Swaying around either side of it, the two silver ships were making it difficult to get a lock on them. Even so, he decided to chance a shot, jamming his thumb down hard on the joystick's trigger. A bright yellow laser beam shot out towards them but missed spectacularly. He fired again, and got the same clumsy result.

'It's no good,' said Max. 'I can't get used to these controls. What I wouldn't give for a games controller right now.'

ED-21 rolled over. 'Your wish is my command, sir.' His eyes swirled and then *ding!* he pulled a controller from out of his chest.

Max looked up at the viewscreen, his jaw clenched with a steely determination. A remarkable transformation had come over him. With a games controller in his hand, Max was no longer a small, timid eleven-year-old boy. Instead, he was an intergalactic fighter pilot who knew no equal.

Suddenly, he saw his chance, and with the deftest of touches, his finger pressed down on the fire button. This time the yellow laser beam scored a direct hit on the lead attacking ship, drilling a neat dinner-plate-sized hole through the exterior of its hull before punching its way out the other side. There was a brief pause, and then the ship seemed to peel apart in a massive explosion of orange and yellow flames.

'YES!' exclaimed Stevie, jumping up and down in celebration.

However, it wasn't over yet. The second attacking ship continued to bear down on its small quarry, but then seemed to think better of it, its thrusters blazing as it turned tail and retreated rapidly into the distance.

'*DeadlyAssassin11* does it again!' shouted out Stevie.

Max let out a huge sigh of relief and slumped back in his chair.

'If I hadn't seen it with my own eyes, I'd never have believed it,' said Lucinda. 'Good work, Pipsqueak.'

'Young master, the ship you have saved is hailing us. Shall I put them on the viewscreen?'

Max looked over to Stevie and Lucinda for confirmation.

'Our first proper aliens,' said Lucinda. 'Why not, they can't be any uglier than this thing here.' She shot Snot a look of disgust as the viewscreen shimmered.

'Greetings, we are the Moleian. I am Gnarl, and this is my brother Gnaw. Thank you for saving us.'

It didn't take a genius to work out how the brothers had come by their names, and Max's attention was immediately drawn to their huge buck teeth, which protruded down over their bottom lips and gave them a somewhat comical appearance. Beady black eyes squinted out from behind folds of wrinkly brown skin, and long wiry whiskers sprouted from small upturned snouts that sniffed constantly at the air. Both were dressed in a type of all-in-one blue boiler suit that zipped tightly up the middle and made the loose skin under their chins bunch up like the bellows of an accordion. In fact, the two were so alike, Max wondered if they might be twins.

'I'm glad we could help,' said Max. 'But if you don't mind me asking, why were those ships chasing you?'

'We were attempting to evade capture,' replied Gnarl, the sagging jowls of skin around his mouth wobbling as he spoke.

'Capture?' said Lucinda suspiciously. 'By who?'

'Why, the Terrasaurs of course. Who else?'

'Er… You'll have to excuse us, but we're not from around here,' said Max.

'But the Terrasaurian Empire controls the whole of this universe,' said Gnarl, scratching his bald head in puzzlement. 'Surely you are aware of them?'

'Let's just say we come from a *very* long way away,' replied Max. 'Please, continue.'

'Very well. The Terrasaurs have enslaved my race so that they may take advantage of our expertise.'

'Expertise? What in, squinting?' whispered Lucinda under her breath.

'Mining, actually,' said Gnarl. 'Our eyesight may be limited, but we have excellent hearing.'

'Please excuse *her*,' said Max. 'Why are the Terrasaurs so desperate for you to mine for them?'

'They force us to mine asteroids for a rare mineral they value above all else. Many of my people have been imprisoned in their labour camps and put to work under their regime.'

'Wait, rewind for a second. This rare mineral, it's not called Multinium, is it?'

'Yes,' replied Gnarl in surprise. 'So, you have heard of that at least.'

'Actually, we're looking for some right now. We need it to power our Multiverse Drive.'

Gnarl leaned in closely to the viewscreen, so that the children could see almost all the way up his snout. '*You* have a Multiverse Drive?' His voice had become almost a whisper. 'Then you are in terrible danger. The Terrasaurs serve the Overlord, a mysterious and power-crazed tyrant whose aim is to control the entire Multiverse. He is thought to be the only one to possess a

Multiverse Drive, but if he discovers that you have your own, then he will stop at nothing to get his hands on it.'

Max turned to the others. 'I told you it was a mistake getting involved.'

'I am sorry to interrupt, young master,' said M.U.M, 'but I detect a fleet of ships heading our way. Estimated time of arrival, two minutes.'

'Forgive us,' said Gnarl. 'By saving my brother and I you have put yourselves in harm's way. It isn't much, but I hope you will accept the Multinium we are beaming to your ship's cargo bay as a token of our thanks. Goodbye my friends, and good luck.'

'No, wait, please. We've so many questions to ask,' pleaded Max.

But it was no use. The viewscreen shimmered to reveal the exterior of Gnarl and Gnaw's ship as it hastily limped into the distance, puffy white clouds of smoke belching out in a trail behind it.

'I can confirm receipt of a small shipment of Multinium,' said M.U.M. 'Unfortunately, there is not enough time for ED-21 to make the necessary repairs to the Multiverse Drive before we are intercepted.'

'Then put your foot on the gas and get us out of here,' said Lucinda, clearly agitated.

'Negative, young miss. This ship is unable to outrun a Crocodile class destroyer.'

'A what?' asked Max.

'The repairs to my matrix are now complete. All information regarding this universe has been downloaded to my data banks. I can confirm that we are being intercepted by a Crocodile class destroyer, the fastest and most heavily armed ship in this universe.'

'Oh, way to go with the timing, M.U.M,' sniped Lucinda, sarcastically clapping her hands together.

'M.U.M, what do we do?' asked Max.

'I am afraid there is nothing that you can do, young master. The alien ship has surrounded itself with a protective energy field. The laser drill would not even dent its hull. I would advise that you surrender.'

'Surrender!' exclaimed Lucinda. 'You're joking, right?'

'I am a computer, young miss. I can assure you, I do not joke.'

'Um, guys. You might want to check this out,' piped up Stevie.

A great hulking brute of a spaceship, flanked by an armada of smaller vessels, took up almost the whole of the viewscreen; a predator, specifically designed to hunt down and destroy its prey. To reinforce this point, as if further proof were needed, it positively bristled with an array of deadly looking weapons, all of which were now trained on the *Cosmo II* and its hapless crew.

'We are receiving an incoming audio message,' said M.U.M.

'ENEMIES OF THE TERRASAURIAN EMPIRE...' roared a rasping voice from out of a speaker.

Snot let out a whimper and jumped up into Stevie's arms.

'PREPARE TO SURRENDER OR BE BLASTED INTO ATOMS! YOU HAVE SIXTY SECONDS TO COMPLY.'

'OK, we need some ideas, and we need them fast,' said Max. Stevie and Lucinda stared back at him with blank expressions. 'Nice work, guys— *not!*' And then he had a brainwave. 'ED-21, you can make just about anything, right?'

'That is correct, sir,' said ED-21, rolling over on his tracks.

'Then how about you make us some weapons to defend ourselves with?'

'Negative, sir. I am afraid my programming will not allow it. However, I would be happy to… happy… happy…'

'Oh no. Not again, not now!' said Lucinda, as ED-21 blew another fuse and slumped forward, tendrils of grey smoke wisping from his head.

'Well, I guess that settles it then, we've no other choice,' said Max. 'M.U.M, contact the other ship.'

'Comms channel open, young master.'

'YOU'VE MADE YOUR CHOICE?' thundered the voice down the speaker.

'Yes,' said Max. 'We surrender.'

The front of the Crocodile class destroyer began to slowly open. Like a fisherman casting a dew-covered net, it fired a sparkling white tractor beam onto the *Cosmo II*, gradually reeling the day's catch into its dark, gaping mouth. Finally, when the helpless ship had been swallowed whole, the jaws of the destroyer snapped shut with a deep, metallic *BOOM!*

CHAPTER SEVEN

THE TERRASAURS

On board the alien ship, the three children were frogmarched along a series of dimly lit corridors until eventually they arrived at a large, cavernous chamber. Here, their captors left them before gradually melting away from sight.

Max squinted in an effort to penetrate the gloom. An orange glow throbbed beneath the steel grating on which he was stood, casting the room in a flickering hellish-coloured light. It was incredibly hot, and plumes of steam rose slowly into the air like ghostly spectres.

'Who dares to fire on my ships?' boomed a voice from out of the shadows. It was accompanied by a waft of evil smelling breath.

The three children stood in a row, trembling.

'I-I-I d-did,' stuttered Max, stepping forward.

'Then you shall die!' growled back the voice.

Out of the murk, stepped what can only be described as something straight from the pages of Max's *Encyclopaedia of Dinosaurs*. It was clearly a Tyrannosaurus Rex, except this one was much smaller than the skeletons Max had seen in the Natural History Museum. Even so, it was still incredibly large and bigger than any human he'd ever seen.

What was really strange though, as if suddenly being confronted with a walking, talking dinosaur wasn't odd enough, was the fact that this one appeared to have squeezed itself into a grand white naval uniform, its gold buttons stretched almost to breaking point over a large pot belly. A scarlet cape draped down majestically from its shoulders onto the floor, and a gaudy gem encrusted crown balanced precariously on top of its bony head.

'*I* am Admiral Tyrannus,' declared the creature pompously. 'Ruler of the Terrasaurian Empire, Emperor of the Four Moons, Divine Majesty of the K'rell System, Grand Duke of the Twin Suns, King of Terra Prime and *conqueror* of this universe.'

'Admiral Fashion Disaster, more like,' whispered Lucinda.

Fortunately, the comment went unnoticed, and Admiral Tyrannus kept his cold, emotionless eyes fixed firmly on Max.

'INSIGNIFICANT VERMIN!' he bellowed. 'Know your place and kneel before me!' A long, scaly green tail whipped out from beneath his cape and, with a flick of his behind, he swept Max's legs from under him so that he landed painfully on his side.

'Hey!' shouted out Stevie, stepping forward.

Admiral Tyrannus turned his attention to Stevie, bending down to offer him an uncomfortably close view of his razor-sharp teeth. Opening his massive jaws, he unfurled an unpleasant looking red forked tongue and proceeded to lick the entire length of the terrified boy's face. 'Hmm... could do with some seasoning, but *you* will make a fine meal.' A great deluge of drool slopped from his mouth and splashed onto the floor. 'Now, where was I before I was so rudely interrupted? Ah yes, the small one.'

His gaze returned to Max who was struggling to his feet. '*You*, however, will need fattening up. Now, tell me who you are and why you attacked my ships.'

Max was trembling so much that he swore he could hear the sound of his own knees knocking together. 'I-I'm Max, Your Majesty, M-Max Voltage. We didn't set out to attack your ships, h-honest. We saw someone in trouble and tried to help them, t-that's all.'

'Then you should be more careful who you choose to help. The Moleian are sworn enemies of the Terrasaurian Empire. Well... what's left of them!' Admiral Tyrannus threw back his head and let out a blood-curdling laugh, seemingly pleased with his own joke. 'I don't recognise your species though,' he said, his eyes narrowing.

'W-We're humans, Your Majesty, from the planet Earth.'

'*Humans?* Hmm... I've heard tell of another like you.'

'You have?' asked Max excitedly. 'Please, we're looking for my...'

'SILENCE! *I* ask the questions. This *Earth*, why haven't I heard of it before? I shall have to conquer it.'

'We come from another universe,' answered Max dejectedly. 'We were trying to repair our Multiverse Drive when you captured us.'

'*Max!*' exclaimed Stevie.

Max had been distracted by the mention of another human. Could it have been his dad? Then he remembered Gnarl's warning about the mysterious Overlord, and he realised he had said too much.

'Your ship is equipped with a Multiverse Drive?' said Admiral Tyrannus, his interest piqued.

Max paused for a second, weighing up his options. It was no good lying now, the damage had already been done. 'Yes,' he replied reluctantly. 'It is.'

'Interesting, *very* interesting. My master will reward me well for your capture.' He clapped his hands together. 'GUARDS!'

Before Max and the others had a chance to protest, they were picked up by the scruffs of their necks and carried unceremoniously from the chamber.

'Be sure to feed up the small one,' called out Admiral Tyrannus after them. 'He's not quite ready for the pot yet.'

He turned to face his guards who were skulking in the background. 'Now, will one of you be a love and turn the lights back on—I can't see past the end of my snout. Oh, and some tea with honey would be lovely; you've no idea how much it hurts my throat to have to shout all the time.'

CHAPTER EIGHT

THE CHOSEN ONE

The iron gate of the cell slammed shut, and the guard turned a rusty key in the lock. The vicious looking horn on the end of his snout, flanked by one either side of his head, instantly identified him as a Triceratops, but this one was walking upright.

'*AATCHOO!*' The guard let out a gargantuan sneeze, removing the two lime green trails of snot that had begun to run down his snout by sweeping his long grey tongue backwards and forwards like a windscreen wiper. '*AATCHOO!*' He sneezed again.

'Here,' said Max, offering the guard his hankie through the metal bars of the cell.

The guard pinched it between two massive fingers and held it closely to his face, seemingly unsure what to do with it.

'For your nose,' said Max, performing an elaborate nose wiping mime.

The guard dabbed hesitantly at his snout. In comparison to his colossal frame, which was largely uncovered apart from an animal hide belted tightly around his waist, the hankie was exceedingly small. But it did the job, and he seemed grateful.

'Allergies,' said the guard through blocked up sinuses. 'Mould spores is making me sneeze a lot.'

Max had seen enough dinosaur movies to recognise that the guard spoke like some kind of prehistoric caveman, and that he wasn't exactly over endowed with brains. He did though, have a point. Every surface of their dark, dingy cell was covered in a creeping carpet of thick green fungus that seemed more suited to a medieval dungeon than an interstellar spaceship.

Giving his snout one loud, final blow, the guard offered the dripping hankie back to Max.

'It's OK,' said Max, politely trying to hide his disgust as he stepped back from the small puddle growing at his feet. 'You can keep it.'

The guard shrugged his shoulders by way of acceptance, wringing out the hankie between his two huge hands before tucking it under his belt.

A gleaming silver ray gun, at odds with its filthy surroundings, was jammed next to it.

'Me Grimhorn,' announced the guard, jabbing a stubby finger into his muscular chest. 'Me's here to make your stay with us a pleasant one.'

'He's joking, right?' asked Lucinda. 'Tell me he's joking.'

Grimhorn wasn't joking.

'You be good now, and everything turn out hunky dory. Well, till boss eats you that is. But don't worry, he make sure you dead first. He not like live food. All that squirming be making a mess of his uniform.'

'Good to know,' said Lucinda sarcastically.

'Grimhorn gots to be going now. Be seeings you in the morning for breakfast.' He slowly trudged off into the darkness, the sound of his sneezing reverberating through the air long after he'd disappeared from sight.

'Way to go, Pipsqueak,' said Lucinda snidely. 'First you hand us over to Admiral Stinky Breath without a fight, and then you go and blab all our secrets.'

Max buried his hands deep into his trouser pockets and stared down awkwardly at his feet, scuffing a shoe against the filthy metal floor. 'Look, I'm sorry, OK. I wasn't thinking properly.'

'Give him a break, Lucinda,' said Stevie. 'I'd like to see how you'd have done. It wasn't that long ago you were crying for your mummy.'

Lucinda let out a snort of derision. 'Here we go again, Bellyache to the rescue. You know, just for once, why don't you let Pipsqueak fight his own battles.'

'It's called being a friend,' retorted Stevie. 'You might want to try it some time.'

'I've got plenty of friends *thank* you very much,' replied Lucinda, crossing her arms defensively.

'Ha!' exclaimed Stevie. 'Friends? You call that little gang of girls you hang around with friends? They're not friends. They're all just as false as you are. Horrible little girls who have to put others down to feel better about themselves. You're pathetic.'

Lucinda looked genuinely shocked. Almost as shocked as Stevie, who couldn't quite believe himself what had just come from his mouth. Even so, he'd meant every word, if not the nasty way in which he'd said them.

'Oh why don't you and your disgusting little pet both go back under the rock you crawled from!' spat out Lucinda, turning her back on him.

Stevie slapped his forehead with the heel of his hand. 'Snot! I'd forgotten all about him. He must still be on board the *Cosmo II*.'

'The filthy little thing probably realised what a loser you are,' said Lucinda, whirling around to face Stevie. Clearly, she wasn't going to allow his verbal assassination of her to go unpunished. 'If it has any sense, it'll get as far away as possible from here and not look back, you… you… stinking great lard bucket!'

As insults go, it wasn't one of her best.

'For months now, I have rotted away in here,' interrupted a croaky voice from a dark corner of the cell, 'and now they add to my torment with a load of bickering younglings.'

All three children jumped in surprise and peered in the direction of the unseen voice. As their eyes gradually adjusted to the darkness, it was just about possible to make out a small figure slumped on the floor, its back propped up against a mould covered wall. It was a Moleian, of that there was no doubt. Even in the darkness, its big buck teeth were an instant giveaway. However, any similarity with Gnarl and Gnaw ended there. Whilst the brothers had looked well fed, podgy even, this one was terribly thin and desperately in need of a good meal.

'You're a Moleian,' said Max.

'Point out the obvious why don't you,' sniped Lucinda.

'Do you always argue as much as this?' asked the Moleian, struggling to stand up.

'Please excuse our rudeness,' said Max, helping him to his feet.

'I am Digger of the, as you say, Moleian.' With some difficulty, he straightened up, brushing himself down in an attempt to appear presentable. A short, withered tail poked pitifully through the remnants of what might once have been a blue boiler suit. 'It appears that you have me at a disadvantage, young one,' he continued, casting his squinting eyes over the three children. 'You are aware of my race, but I am not familiar with yours.'

'We've encountered your race before,' said Max. 'We helped two Moleian to escape from the Terrasaurs. That's how we ended up stuck in here.'

'Then I am in debt to you for saving my comrades. Please, consider me your loyal servant.' He attempted to solemnly bow, clutching the small of his back and grimacing as he did so. He was obviously in some discomfort.

'Really, you don't owe us anything,' said Max. '*Although*, there is one way you might be able to help us.'

The group found a corner of the cell where the ceiling wasn't dripping and sat down on the damp, grimy floor. All except Lucinda, who eyed it disdainfully. Stevie produced a chocolate bar from his coat pocket and gave it to Digger, watching in amazement as the Moleian pushed it through his buck teeth like a log through a wood chipper. Within a matter of seconds, he'd devoured it completely, beckoning for another as he listened intently to Max's incredible story. M.U.M activating the Multiverse Drive, his missing dad, their encounter with Gnarl and Gnaw. Max left nothing out.

'Well, you really are in a pickle,' said Digger, licking the chocolate from his whiskers. 'But how can *I* help you?'

'You can tell us what you know,' replied Max. 'Gnarl talked about an Overlord, who is he?'

'A better question might be *what* is he?' said Digger. 'No one knows for sure, for no one who has seen him in person has ever lived to tell the tale. But I shall come back to that later. First, you must understand that this universe was once a peaceful and pleasant place in which to live. My people and the other species in it prospered, and we lived in harmony with the Terrasaurs. They have always been an aggressive race, but they generally kept their fighting amongst themselves. You may have noticed, but they are not the most intelligent of creatures.'

'Yeah, I kind of got that impression,' said Max.

'Then one day, out of the blue, the Overlord appeared in a ship so huge that it blocked the light from the stars themselves.'

Max's eyes widened.

'Remember, young one, the Overlord has amassed a myriad of different technologies from many different universes, making him incredibly powerful. He chose to demonstrate this by making an example of a large planet called Nibulis IV, homeworld to the Nibuli. Its ruler had dared to speak out against the Overlord—a fatal mistake. As punishment, the Overlord deployed one of his more unusual weapons, a miniaturisation ray, which he used to reduce the huge planet to the size of a marble in a matter of seconds. It is said that he had the planet brought before him, crushing it to dust under his foot.'

A hush came over the group as the children tried to comprehend such a thing. A whole planet and its people destroyed in the blink of an eye, and in such a bizarre manner. Naturally, it fell to Lucinda to break the silence with one of her trademark quips.

'So where does Admiral Dino-Bore and his army of grunts fit into all of this?'

Digger gave a wry smile. 'The Overlord preyed on the Terrasaurs' stupidity and greed, promising them great riches and power beyond their wildest dreams in return for their obedience. They agreed, and with the help of the Overlord's advanced technology, they set about enslaving the people of this universe. Any of us that did not capitulate were exterminated or forced to seek refuge amongst the stars. Do not be fooled by their lack of intelligence.

Great power in the hands of the ignorant is the greatest threat of all.'

'So let me get this right,' said Max. 'Each time the Overlord jumps to another universe, he bribes the most aggressive species in it to do his dirty work.'

'Correct,' replied Digger. 'Then, when he has stripped that universe of anything of value, he moves on to the next, leaving a trail of chaos and destruction in his wake. His only concern is to satisfy his thirst for Multinium and to power his Multiverse Drive, for without it, his power is greatly diminished.'

'But how is any of this possible? My dad invented the Multiverse Drive, and he went missing before even our own government could use it. How can the Overlord also have one?'

'So many questions, young one. Find your father, and you will find the answers that you seek. But be warned though, this is a dangerous path to follow, one that will put you and your friends' lives in great peril.'

'I'll do *anything* to find my dad,' said Max defiantly. 'Whatever it takes.'

'Count me in,' said Stevie enthusiastically.

That just left Lucinda.

'If you are to have any chance of success, then you must all work together,' said Digger, looking up at Lucinda who was still quietly seething from Stevie's comments earlier.

'What chance do we have?' asked Lucinda, dramatically throwing her arms up in the air. 'We couldn't even outrun an overgrown lizard. Why don't we try to make a deal with this Overlord instead? Who knows, we might even get rewarded for it.'

'Then you have failed before you have even begun,' said Digger mournfully.

'No,' said Max. 'We'll do this with or *without* Lucinda's help.'

'Then you must know your enemy,' said Digger. 'I told you before that no one who has seen the Overlord in person has ever lived to tell the tale. Well, that is not strictly true. There is one.'

'*You?*' asked Max.

'Yes, young one. I know it is hard to imagine looking at me now, but I was once a resistance fighter, and quite a successful one at that, if I may say so. I commanded a small group of

Moleian that targeted lone Terrasaurian ships, trying to cause as much disruption as we could. On one such raid, we had one of their cargo ships in our laser sights. We were about to attack it, when from behind a planetary moon appeared a huge fleet of Terrasaurian ships. It was a trap; we had been betrayed. The Terrasaurs had been waiting for us all along.'

'Betrayed?' asked Max. 'By who?'

'I never found out. It may even have been by one of my own people, for the right price. It seems that I was considered important enough to have a bounty placed on my head, and when I was captured I was brought before the Overlord himself.' Digger paused, reliving the moment in his head. 'Are you sure you want me to continue?' he asked. 'It is not for the faint-hearted.'

'Best not continue then,' said Lucinda mockingly.

'We can handle it, can't we, Stevie?' said Max.

Stevie nodded hesitantly.

'Then I shall proceed. Before I was presented to him, I was thrown into a holding cell filled with many different races. They were resistance fighters like myself, separated by space and time, but all with one common purpose. The tale they had to tell was a very strange one. Put simply, the Overlord is an abomination of nature. Whatever he once may have been no longer exists. For every universe that he has conquered, he has stolen their technology, but not just to further his own power. No, he wants more than that. He is on a quest to become immortal.'

'Immortal? But that's not possible,' said Max disbelievingly. 'No one can live forever.'

'You know that, and I know that,' said Digger. 'But the Overlord does not think like us. I am afraid he is quite insane. He has *recruited* the finest medical minds from across the Multiverse, forcing them to perform countless operations on him. They augment his body with mechanical implants and inject him with supposed elixirs of youth. Most horrific of all though, they replace his ageing body parts with the limbs and organs of the species he has conquered.'

'And you have seen this?' asked Max.

'I saw something. The room I was brought to was dark, and as you know, my eyesight is not the best. Whispers circulate that the Overlord's body has begun to reject all the operations and transplants he has had, and that bright light hurts his eyes and burns his skin. As a result, he wears a hooded black robe that covers him almost entirely from head to toe. When I saw him, he was sat on a mechanical throne, which seemed to double up as a type of life support system. A multitude of clear, transparent tubes sprouted from it, disappearing beneath his cloak, and every now and again they would shudder as a foul green liquid was sucked through them. I assumed they were removing the poisons created by his rapidly decaying body.'

'Did you see his face?' asked Stevie, fascinated and repulsed in equal measure.

'No, the hood from his cloak cast his face into shadow, making it impossible to discern his features. However, I did see his hands resting on the throne's armrests. One was covered in a thick blue fur, whilst the other was pale and skeletal with long, overgrown nails that had started to curl at the ends. I could not tell you which one was his own, and which one was a transplant. Indeed, it is possible that he was born with neither.'

'Did he speak to you?' asked Max. 'What did he sound like?'

Digger shuddered at the memory. 'Imagine if evil itself could talk. *That* is what he sounded like. He told me I had been quite a thorn in his side, and that my raids on his ships had seriously disrupted his deliveries of Multinium. As a result, he chose to punish me, but rather than have me executed, he handed me back to the Terrasaurs instead. It amuses him to know that they have me locked away in here, facing a slow and prolonged death.' Digger held out his skinny arms and shook his head forlornly.

'So, he's like, a total freak then,' said Lucinda. 'A planet destroying, universe ending, big ol' fruit loop. You guys must be even crazier than he is if you think you can take him on.'

But Lucinda's comments had gone unnoticed. Digger had closed his eyes, as if lost in deep thought. 'There is an ancient prophecy amongst my people,' he suddenly announced. 'It tells of an unlikely hero, one from far away who shall defeat the Overlord and unite the Multiverse in peace.'

His eyes flicked open, and he looked directly at Max. 'I believe that *you* are the chosen one.'

'Whoa! Hold on just one minute, Goofy Gob,' said Lucinda. 'If you think Pipsqueak here is the *chosen one,* then being cooped up in this cell on your own for so long has clearly scrambled your brain. The only thing he's good at is playing video games, and I reckon it's going to take a lot more than a kid with a games controller in his hand to become the hero you're looking for.'

'I hate to say it, but she's got a point,' said Max. 'What difference can *I* make?'

'No one sets out to be a hero, young one,' said Digger. 'Circumstances dictate that. Remember, you possess the greatest threat the Overlord has ever faced—your own Multiverse Drive. With that, and a little faith in yourself, anything is possible.'

'I've got faith in you,' said Stevie. 'Even if *others* haven't.' He pulled a face at Lucinda, who sneered back at him.

Max smiled. He knew that Stevie would do anything for him, even if it meant giving his life, and that he in turn would do anything for him.

'What if we do nothing?' he asked. 'What if we do what Lucinda said and try to make a deal with the Overlord?'

'The Overlord does not make deals,' said Digger. 'When you are as powerful as he is, you do not need to. Do nothing, and he will take your Multiverse Drive and add it to his own. He will become twice as powerful. Then, the day will come when he makes the jump to your own universe, and your people will succumb to the same fate as mine. It is only a matter of time.'

Max let out a long sigh. 'I was afraid you were going to say that.' He couldn't ignore the nagging feeling at the back of his mind that his dad was involved in all of this, but how? There was only one way to find out.

'OK,' said Max. 'Let's do it.'

CHAPTER NINE
A STARTLING DISCOVERY

'Where's my make-up artist?' bellowed Admiral Tyrannus. 'Take the shine off my forehead! I need to look my best!'

'Me coming, boss,' said a guard, his arms overflowing with a variety of strange smelling creams and powders. Like Grimhorn, he and his fellow guards were all walking, talking Triceratops. Perhaps slightly cleverer, but not much.

'Medal shiner!'

'Here, boss,' said another guard. 'Me good spit n' polish.' He produced a dirty cloth and made an unpleasant gurgling sound in the back of his throat as he hawked up a great gob of phlegm. Unfortunately though, his aim was off, and it missed the medals pinned to the Admiral's chest completely, landing instead on his snout before slowly dripping off the end of it.

'IDIOT!' roared Admiral Tyrannus, batting away the guard with his tail.

A third guard operated a computer console and was haphazardly twiddling a bewildering number of knobs and switches. 'Communications array ready to come online, boss. Going live in five… four… um… one… um… *two?*'

'Tyrannus!' hissed a hooded, shadowy figure from a large screen on the wall. 'This had better be important or I'll have you stuffed and put on display here in my throne room.'

It was the Overlord. He was sat on his throne and cast, almost entirely, in silhouette against a dim blue background.

'I'm sorry to disturb you, master,' grovelled Admiral Tyrannus. He attempted to kneel down in reverence, pretending not to notice as the seat of his overly tight trousers tore loudly down the middle. 'However, there's been a most interesting development.'

'Spit it out, Tyrannus. I've better things to do with my time than stare at your ugly mug.'

'Of course, my master. A thousand apologies. I thought you should know, I've captured a young boy and his two accomplices. He says that they come from a planet called Earth.'

'*Earth!*' screeched the Overlord.

'Yes, master. You've heard of it?'

'I'm aware of it. Never forget, Tyrannus—I'm aware of *everything*. Is this why you've dared to contact me?'

'No, there is more, master. The boy claims his ship has a Multiverse Drive.'

'WHAT!' raged the Overlord, slamming down an orange feathered fist onto his throne's armrest. His surgeons had obviously been busy since Digger had last seen him. 'You've confirmed this?'

'My men are attempting to access their ship now, master. We have it in our docking bay. It appears to have somehow locked itself, but it's only a matter of time before we gain entry.'

'This boy, does he have a name?'

'Voltage, master. Max Voltage.'

For the briefest of moments, Admiral Tyrannus could have sworn that he saw a flash of red from beneath the Overlord's cowl, but he quickly dismissed it as interference from the array.

'And how do you know this Max Voltage speaks the truth?'

'He mistakenly divulged the information

during interrogation, master. I don't believe he is lying.'

'You've done well, Tyrannus. Maybe your race aren't so stupid after all. I've grown tired of this universe and had planned to move on, but this changes everything. Engage your hyperdrive, I shall rendezvous with you at Terra Prime in two days.'

'Yes, master. It shall be done.'

'Do not fail me, Tyrannus. Do what you want with the other two, but I want this Max Voltage alive. And whatever happens, do *not* touch the Multiverse Drive. Am I making myself clear, or do I need to remind you what happens to those that displease me?'

Admiral Tyrannus gulped loudly. 'No, master. That won't be necessary.'

'Good. It just so happens that I've recently acquired a roll of the finest Sirellian silk. An interesting species of master tailors, very nimble hands. I believe I owned one once.' The Overlord slowly flexed the fingers of 'his' orange feathered hand. 'Hmm… maybe it's time for a change? Do this successfully, Tyrannus, and the silk is yours. No doubt, you can have it made into another of those *pretty* little uniforms of yours.'

'You're too kind, master.'

'Now go, I...' The Overlord suddenly stopped mid-sentence, his body gripped by a violent seizure. Thrashing around in his throne, the convulsions only stopped when a mysterious figure appeared from off-screen and plunged a long hypodermic needle into the shadowed crook of the Overlord's neck.

Abruptly, the transmission ended.

'Did you hear that?' said Admiral Tyrannus, turning to his guards. 'Sirellian silk! Oh goody, goody, goody!' He jumped up and down, clapping his hands together like an excitable little girl who had just received a cute, fluffy kitten for her birthday. 'I will be the best dressed dinosaur in the *whole* universe!'

The three guards looked on in bemusement as Admiral Tyrannus danced around the room. Considering his huge size, he was remarkably light on his feet.

'Oh, and of course, there'll be lots of death and destruction along the way,' he added gruffly, noticing the smirks on the guards' faces. 'Now, lay in a course for Terra Prime, I don't want *anything* to spoil this for me.'

'So that's it then, that's our escape plan,' said Max, looking up at the others. He'd used his finger to draw a crude map of the interior of the ship in the dirt on the floor of their cell.

'Not so much a plan, more a suicide mission,' said Lucinda, raising an eyebrow dubiously. 'This map of yours is based on memory. One wrong turn and we're mincemeat. And I don't know about you, but I don't fancy ending up being pooped out of a dinosaur's flabby bottom.'

'The cynical one is right,' said Digger. 'It is too risky. Sleep now, young ones. With a new day will come a new plan.'

'*Ow!*' exclaimed Stevie unexpectedly. He was holding his nose and wincing in pain.

'What is it, Stevie?' asked Max, a concerned look on his face.

'It's my nose; it feels like there's something stuck up it.'

Lucinda pulled a face. 'Gross. You sure it's not your finger? It usually is.'

But there was no reply from Stevie, and the small group looked on in horror as his nose began to vigorously twitch from side to side. Slowly, his left nostril started to expand and what looked like a giant green bogey began to emerge.

'Ew! I told you if you kept picking it that one day your brain would fall out,' said Lucinda grimacing.

By now, Stevie's nostril had become so big that he could probably have put his whole fist up there, let alone a finger. Then, *PLOP!* Snot fell to the floor in a slimy mucous covered heap.

'Snot!' said Stevie, wrinkling his nose as his nostril returned to its normal size. 'Here boy.' Snot yipped in excitement, jumping up into his master's arms. 'He must've hidden up there when we were captured. Can't say I noticed.'

'You were probably eating something at the time,' sneered Lucinda.

'Digger, this is Snot,' declared Stevie proudly.

Digger nodded at Snot. 'A strange creature to be sure, but a welcome one. Now, enough excitement. I am tired and need my sleep. Let us rest and begin afresh tomorrow.'

Using their coats as pillows, Max and Stevie lay side by side on the soiled floor of the cell,

Snot curled up at their feet. Digger lay alongside them, whilst Lucinda remained detached from the group and huddled in a corner on her own. Slowly, one by one, they fell asleep, until the only sound that could be heard was their snoring—and the occasional fart from Stevie.

Max.

Several hours passed by. Whilst the others appeared to be in a deep slumber, Max tossed and turned in his sleep, as if experiencing a bad dream.

Max.

Disturbing images floated around his unconscious mind, terrible visions of death and destruction. Briefly, his dad's grinning face appeared, only to melt away and be replaced by the image of a hooded figure who began to laugh maniacally. Reaching up, it went to pull back its black cowl and reveal its face…

Young Master Max! Wake up!

The urgency of the words popped the image as if it were a bubble, and Max woke with a start.

Young master. Can you hear me?

M.U.M, is that you? asked Max, rubbing his eyes. But the words that came out didn't come from his mouth. They came from within his head.

Yes, young master. Are you OK?

I'm fine, I think. But how's this possible?

Do you remember what I said to you before, about the cybernetic link that I share with you and your father? I am using it now.

That's incredible. You mean we can have a whole conversation in my head?

That is correct. Think what you want to say, and I will hear you as clearly as if you had spoken the words themselves. More importantly though, it means that I can help you to escape. Now, we must hurry. Tell me everything that has happened so far.

As the rest slept on, Max recounted the events on board Admiral Tyrannus's ship, marvelling at the strange new form of communication. Every now and again, M.U.M would ask questions, and in turn, she would divulge information to him. Max learnt that in this universe, the dinosaurs of ancient Earth had never been wiped out by an asteroid. As a result, humankind had never existed, and the dinosaurs had evolved into the semi-intelligent species the children had encountered.

I am afraid there has been a rather disturbing development, young master. I have managed to access the destroyer's computer. You are being taken to Terra Prime, to be handed over to the Overlord.

Terra Prime?

The Terrasaurs' home world, or as we know it—Earth. If this happens, then the odds of a successful escape attempt are greatly reduced. If you would like, I can calculate them for you?

Max heard himself laughing in his head. *No, that's OK. I can pretty much guess they're not great. Well then, we'd better get moving. It's time to wake the others.*

CHAPTER TEN

THE GREAT ESCAPE

'So M.U.M's, like, in your head right now?' asked Lucinda. She was stood with her back to the others, gripping the iron bars of the cell like a particularly sorrowful looking zoo exhibit.

'Not *right* now,' said Max. 'But if I concentrate hard enough and focus my mind, then I can talk to her.'

'This M.U.M, she can help us?' asked Digger, grooming his whiskers.

'She's managed to hack this ship's computer and download a map of it,' said Max. 'When I ask her to, she can project an image of the map into my mind and guide us safely back to the *Cosmo II*.'

'Can't she just beam us out of here using that teleport gizmo?' asked Lucinda, although the thought of having her atoms scrambled secretly filled her with dread.

'I've already thought of that,' replied Max, 'but M.U.M says it's being blocked somehow.'

'So it's up to us to escape, right?' said Stevie.

Right on cue, Grimhorn appeared at the iron bars of the cell. 'Mornings,' he said, a cheerful smile on his face. He removed a large bunch of jangling keys from a hook on his belt and unlocked the iron gate, swinging it back with a loud *CLANG!* 'Breakfast is being served. You not make mess now.' He threw down a large bowl of brown slop onto the floor. At first glance, it appeared to be spaghetti, but closer inspection revealed it to be a mass of squirming worm-like creatures—which were still *very* much alive.

'Don't you have anything less… *wriggly*?' demanded Lucinda, recoiling from the bowl as one of the worms made a bid for freedom over the side.

'You is being lucky,' said Grimhorn. 'Pus Worms be especially delicious this time of year.' He slammed the iron gate shut behind him and was about to turn the key in the lock, when he doubled over in a sudden fit of sneezes. '*AATCHOO!*'

Lucinda cried out in horror as a large blob of shiny green snot trickled slowly between her eyes and down the bridge of her nose.

'Oops! Sorry 'bout that,' said Grimhorn, wiping his nose on the back of his hand. 'Be seeings you later.' He pulled the key from the lock, tunelessly whistling and spinning the bunch of keys around a finger as he slowly waddled away.

'Did you see that?' said Digger, trying to contain his excitement.

'See what?' exclaimed Lucinda. 'I can't see anything through all this snot!'

'I saw it,' said Max, rising to his feet. 'I don't think Grimhorn turned the key.' To test his theory, he walked over to the iron gate, gently nudging it with the flat of his hand. Sure enough, it swung open ever so slightly, creaking as it did so. Max winced at the sound, and everyone held their breath as they waited to see if Grimhorn would come running back. What felt like an eternity passed, but there was no sign of movement. Grimhorn's ears were as blocked as his nostrils.

'Well, what are we waiting for?' asked Stevie, breaking the silence. 'Let's get out of here.'

A serious look came over Digger's face. 'Once you step outside of these walls, there is no going back. You are quite sure that this is the path you wish to take?'

'We have to try,' said Max. 'You said it yourself. If we do nothing, then we're all doomed anyhow.'

Digger took Max's hand and slowly raised himself from the floor. 'Then so be it. I am with you, young ones. I may be weak, but there is fight left in me yet.'

'It'll be just like a video game,' said Stevie. 'Admiral Tyrannus is just an end of level baddie who needs to be defeated.'

'That just leaves you,' said Max, turning to Lucinda. 'Are you with us?'

Lucinda groaned. 'Talk about being stuck between a rock and a hard place.' She took a couple of steps towards Max, so that their noses were almost touching, and looked him directly in the eyes. 'Promise me I won't end up as dinosaur droppings.'

'You know I can't make that promise,' said Max. 'But I promise you this. If you do stay here, then your chances of being scraped off the bottom of someone else's shoe are even greater.'

Lucinda laughed nervously. 'Not exactly the stirring speech I was hoping for from the *saviour* of the Multiverse. You might want to work on that.'

Digger hobbled over to the iron gate. 'Young ones, we must hurry,' he urged. 'The time to act is now.'

'Why do I get the feeling I'm going to regret this?' said Lucinda. She gestured to Max with her arm, as if to say 'after you,' and the small group slipped silently one by one through the iron gate.

'Um, aren't you forgetting something, Butterball?' whispered Lucinda.

Stevie looked at her, unsure what she meant.

'Green, slimy, even more disgusting than you are…?'

'Doh! Of course. Snot, here boy!' Snot zoomed from out of the shadows, wheezing excitedly at his master's feet.

Lucinda shook her head in despair, and the group proceeded to make their way slowly down the poorly lit corridor. As they did so, they passed cell after cell of all manner of curious looking creatures, a menagerie of different species that, with the Overlord's help, had been imprisoned by the Terrasaurs.

'Talk about a freak show,' said Lucinda, batting away a long tentacle that had meandered its way through the iron bars of one of the cells.

'Just because they are different from what *you* consider to be normal, does not make them freaks,' said Digger. 'You are too quick to judge what you do not understand.'

A low murmur had started up. Dozens of different languages were chattering away excitedly as the creatures in the cells began to realise what was happening.

But it may have been premature. As the group reached the end of the corridor, they were confronted by a heavy iron door. On the wall next to it, partially hidden under a thick layer of grime and mould, was a control panel. A four-digit number was required if the door was to open.

'I could contact M.U.M?' said Max. 'See if she can crack the code.'

'No need,' replied Lucinda. She casually punched 1–2–3–4 into the control panel, and the iron door suddenly shot up like the portcullis of a castle.

'How did you know?' asked Stevie, quietly impressed.

'It doesn't take a genius to work it out, Chubba Chops,' replied Lucinda. 'We're not exactly dealing with the brightest bunch. 1–2–3–4 was the obvious choice.'

Digger looked at Max. 'If this M.U.M of yours is going to help us, then now is the time.'

Max closed his eyes, his brow furrowing in concentration. *M.U.M, are you there?*

I am here, young master.

I need that map of the ship, and I need it now!

Almost instantly, a three-dimensional image of the ship's interior appeared in Max's mind, as clear as if he were holding a map in his hand.

Max looked at the others. 'Ready?'

'As we'll ever be,' replied Lucinda.

'Right then. Let's go!'

CHAPTER ELEVEN

SNOT TO THE RESCUE

'Take a left,' whispered Max.

With Digger leading, the group crept slowly down the corridor, although it was more like a sewer. Water constantly dripped from the ceiling, and a small stream of scummy water trickled around their feet. According to M.U.M, they were located deep within the bowels of the ship. If they were to make it to the docking bay, and the safety of the *Cosmo II,* they would first to have to negotiate a network of dark passages, the dim bunker lights along the walls barely lighting their way.

'What's with the low-tech?' asked Lucinda, brushing a cobweb out of her path. She only just managed to contain a shriek of horror as a ten-legged spider dangled down in front of her, clearly taking offence at having just had its home destroyed.

'The Terrasaurs are not a technologically minded race,' replied Digger over his shoulder. 'This ship and everything in it was gifted to them by the Overlord, one of his many, shall we say, *acquisitions*. They lack the intelligence to maintain it, and certain parts of the ship have fallen into disrepair, hence our current surroundings. If it was not for the Overlord, they would still be in the Dark Ages.'

The group pressed on, Digger continuing to scout ahead. Every now and again, they came to a junction, and Max would consult the map in his head before giving directions. They appeared to be making good progress, when Digger suddenly stopped dead in his tracks. He raised a hand, and the others came to a halt behind him.

'What is it?' whispered Max.

'Footsteps,' replied Digger. 'Coming this way.'

Max listened intently, but all he could hear was the sound of Stevie's belly rumbling behind him. He was about to question whether Digger was imagining things, when he heard it, the faint but unmistakable sound of huge dinosaur feet plodding their way towards them. A low, and very familiar, disgruntled murmuring accompanied it.

'Grimhorn, do this. Grimhorn, do that. Grimhorn dropped on head as baby. Bloomin' boss. Me tell him what he can do with job.' A series of ferocious sounding sneezes followed in quick succession.

'Sounds like our *friend* from the cell block,' whispered Lucinda. 'What are we going to do now?'

'We can turn back and find another way,' said Digger, turning to the children. 'Or, we can stand and fight.'

The three children looked at one another, no one wanting to commit to a plan of action. Again, it was up to Max to take the lead.

'We stand and fight,' he said boldly, much to the surprise of Stevie and Lucinda. 'What? Why are you both looking at me like that? If we run away every time we bump into someone, then we'll never get off this ship.'

For once, Lucinda looked impressed. 'Maybe you've the makings of a hero after all, Pipsqueak.'

Max stood side by side with Digger. In a matter of seconds, Grimhorn would be upon them. Their only chance was to take him by surprise, but that was looking increasingly unlikely as Snot began to yip loudly at their feet.

'Snot, quiet!' urged Stevie. But Snot continued yipping.

Stevie was about to pick him up, when something amazing happened. Before their very eyes, Snot stretched and expanded into an exact replica of one of the guards, albeit with a slightly green hue. It was as if someone had poured him into a giant guard shaped jelly mould.

'Whoa, cool!' exclaimed Stevie. 'Snot can shapeshift!'

But he would have to put his excitement on hold, for there standing in front of the group, was a very befuddled looking Grimhorn.

'What going on here?' he asked, apparently fooled by Snot's disguise. 'Me not know boss wants to see prisoners?'

'*Bleurgh!*' replied Snot.

'Bleurgh?' asked Grimhorn. 'What bleurgh mean?'

'*Bleurgh!*' said Snot again.

'Oh, me gets it now, you not feel well. Yeah, me feel pretty bleurgh too. You do look bit green round gills if honest.'

'*Bleurgh!*'

'Yeah, yeah. Boss not tell Grimhorn anything. Miserable ol' skinflint. Best not be late now or he gets *real* mad. Me hopes you feel better.' And with that, he let the group pass. As he waddled his way into the gloom, his stumpy tail flicked up, and he let off a firecracker of a fart that sent a blast of warm air hurtling back down the corridor.

'Ew! Rotten eggs!' exclaimed Lucinda, her pigtails blowing back under the force of the foul gust of 'wind'.

'Oops! Sorry!' called back Grimhorn. 'Food here not agree with me.' As the darkness began to swallow him up, a series of smaller farts trumpeted from his behind, each one punctuated by an exclamation of surprise and an apology.

'Snot, do something,' muttered Stevie. 'He'll soon work out that something's not right.'

Lucinda looked at him doubtfully.

'OK, well maybe not soon, but *eventually* he'll work it out, and then we'll be for it.'

Snot let out an ear-splitting '*BLEURGH!*' and Grimhorn came running back.

'What wrong, friend?'

Snot lifted his right 'arm' and bopped Grimhorn on the head with a clenched up fist.

'Ow! That not nice. What you do that for?' asked Grimhorn, rubbing his head.

Snot raised his arm again, but this time his fist changed shape into a huge mallet, which he promptly brought crashing down on top of Grimhorn's thick bonce.

'*Ouuchhh…*' slurred Grimhorn. He stood there for a moment, the message to his pea-sized brain to fall over unconscious not immediately computing. Several seconds passed before his eyes finally crossed, and he toppled like a felled oak tree onto the floor.

'Quick, get his ray gun,' said Digger.

Max crouched down to check on Grimhorn. He may have been their jailer, but he was harmless enough. Fortunately, he was snoring soundly, the throbbing welt on his head meaning he would wake up with an almighty headache, but nothing more.

Satisfied there was no lasting damage, Max hastily pulled the ray gun from under Grimhorn's belt. 'Let me guess, another *acquisition?*' He tucked it into the waistband of his trousers, pulling down his top over the grip so that it was hidden from sight.

'You learn fast, young one,' replied Digger. 'Luckily for us, it was not made for dinosaur-sized hands.'

The group continued onwards. Using Snot as cover, they passed several guards who all grunted in greeting as they walked by, little suspecting that a jailbreak was in progress. Gradually, the corridors became wider and lighter, and they soon found themselves sweltering under harsh strip lighting that beat down like a desert sun.

'Why's it so hot?' asked Stevie, who had been reduced to a walking puddle. Not even one of his dad's famous 'Bottom Burner' curries made him sweat this much.

'Think about it,' replied Max, wiping the sweat from his brow. 'You remember that pet Iguana I used to have, the one you *accidentally* let escape? It had a sunlamp in its tank. Lizards like the heat, and I'm guessing the Terrasaurs are no different.'

Stevie took off his coat and began tugging at his t-shirt. 'Maybe I'll feel cooler if I take off some clothes.'

'Stop right there, Porky Chops!' said Lucinda. 'The t-shirt stays on or being eaten alive will be the least of your worries, believe me.'

Max laughed and shook his head. Stevie and Lucinda had become quite the double act. Who knows, if they got out of this mess with their lives, then they might even end up as friends one day. Or had the heat made him delirious?

There was no time to ponder further as the group approached a crossroads. It was becoming obvious they were getting near to the nerve centre of the ship, and that their chances of being discovered were increasing with every step.

'Which way, young one?' asked Digger.

Max furrowed his brow. Nothing. He tried again. Still nothing.

'What's with the delay, Pipsqueak? Get a move on,' said Lucinda impatiently.

'I… I'm having problems contacting M.U.M. She's stopped projecting the map into my mind.'

He tried again, this time furrowing his brow so hard that he thought his head might explode. It was futile. For some reason the link between them had been broken, and it had happened at the worst possible time.

Digger sniffed at the air nervously. 'Quickly, we must make a decision.'

'L-Left,' said Max uncertainly. 'Take a left.'

'Face it, we're lost,' said Lucinda.

It certainly looked that way. The group had been wandering the corridors aimlessly for the last twenty minutes, Max still unable to make contact with M.U.M. He was about to try again, when a door slid open, and a guard stepped straight into their path.

'What you doing here?' asked the guard. 'You know prisoners not allowed—restricted access.' He pointed to a large sign on the wall. It was actually the sign for the toilets, but now didn't seem an appropriate time to point out his mistake.

The group looked to Snot to respond, but no 'bleurgh' was forthcoming. Instead, he started to vigorously shiver and shake, like a jelly being wobbled on a plate. His head, which had served as a passable impersonation of a Triceratops, suddenly inflated to grotesque proportions before rapidly shrinking down to the size of a tennis ball.

'W-What happening?' asked the guard, recoiling in a mixture of terror and disgust.

Snot's inability to hold his shape quickly spread to the rest of his body. One moment he was blown up like a blimp, and then the next he was like a shrivelled party balloon. Finally, when he could hold out no more, he shrank back to his recognisable self and fell with a *SPLAT!* to the floor. Letting out a whimper, he shot over to Stevie and cowered behind his master's ankles. There were clearly limitations to his shapeshifting skills.

'Hmm… Sumthink very wrong 'bout all this,' said the guard, scratching his head.

Max could almost hear the cogs of the guard's brain slowly creak into action as he tried to figure out what was happening. And the group may even have got away with it, had one of them thought up a half decent excuse. At least they might have done if, at that exact moment, the ship's alarm hadn't also gone off, accompanied by the nasal tones of a certain guard over the speaker system.

'Alert… *AATCHOO!*… Alert. Is this thing working? Escaped prisoners, repeating, escaped prisoners. Not nice. Hit Grimhorn on head. Be approaching with caution. *AATCHOO!*'

Max looked calmly at the others. 'Well, I guess this might be a good time to…'

'RUN!' shouted Lucinda, pushing Max out the way as she fled down the corridor. The others followed closely behind, leaving the guard to continue scratching his head as he watched them disappear into the distance. Eventually, the penny dropped.

'Oh, me gets it now,' he said. 'Come back! Me promise not to hurt you. Well… not much.'

CHAPTER TWELVE

POWER UP!

'What do you mean the prisoners have escaped?'
raged Admiral Tyrannus. He was stood in front
of a full-length mirror and was busy admiring
his reflection from a variety of different angles.
Alongside him was a tall ladder, and a small
rodent-like creature was busy scuttling up
and down it with a long measuring tape and
a mouthful of pins. The Admiral was being
measured for his new uniform.

'Um, Grimhorn left cell unlocked, boss,'
replied the guard nervously. 'He being treated by
Nursie now for nasty bump on head.'

'GRIMHORN! What idiot put him in charge of
the cell block?'

'Um, you did, boss. You demoted him after his
last mishap. It was either that or toilet cleaner.'

'*Whaaaat?*'

'Oh, er… what I meant to say was, *I* did boss,' spluttered the guard. 'Yes, it was all *my* fault.'

'You bet it was. Can't you do anything right!'

'Um, I don't know, boss. Can't I?'

'IDIOT! It was a rhetorical question, you don't need to answer it. I'm sure even you and your witless cronies can round up a handful of children. You can do that, can't you?'

The guard remained silent and stared blankly ahead. After a long pause, Admiral Tyrannus threw back his head in despair and let out a long, guttural sigh.

'OK, that one *wasn't* rhetorical.'

'Oh. Yeah, boss. No problem, boss.'

'Good. And by the way, make sure you don't kill them, especially the small one. I want them alive, for now at least. Maybe just separate them from a limb or two. Now, get out of my sight and don't disturb me again until they've been caught.'

'Okey dokey, boss.' The guard bowed and scraped in a grovelling fashion as he clumsily backed out of the room.

Admiral Tyrannus went back to admiring his reflection in the mirror. Sucking in his belly, he looked back over his shoulder and addressed his tiny tailor. 'Now, tell me honestly. Does my bum look big to you?'

'It's no good, we're pinned down!' shouted Max, flinching as a dazzling golden laser beam sizzled just millimetres above his head.

The group were trapped in a large storage area, crouched down behind several tall metal barrels that leaked a foul smelling, purple-coloured sludge onto the floor.

'The ray gun!' shouted Digger. 'Give me the ray gun!'

Max pulled the ray gun from the waistband of his trousers and passed it to Digger who cautiously peered over the top of a barrel. Even with his poor eyesight, he could clearly see at least three guards spread out around the room. To say they were hidden would be incorrect, and had it been a game of hide and seek, the guards would definitely have lost. One was stooped behind a tall pile of wooden crates in the far-left corner of the room, whilst another was slouched behind some more barrels to the right. In the middle, a bandage wrapped tightly around his head, was Grimhorn, who was under the mistaken belief that if he stood really still without blinking, then no one could see him.

He really was *very* stupid.

Suddenly, a laser beam shot from the direction of the crates, and Digger was forced to duck back down behind the safety of the barrels.

'Come out!' shouted one of the guards. 'With your… um… feet in the air!'

Unsurprisingly, the group remained where they were.

'We not want to kill you,' called out another guard. 'Come out now, and we even let you keep all your arms and legs.'

Digger went to raise the ray gun but found that his stick-thin arms no longer possessed the strength. 'It is no good, I am too weak,' he said, offering the ray gun to Max. 'You will have to try instead.'

'Me?' replied Max, startled.

'Come on, Pipsqueak,' said Lucinda. 'You can't chicken out now.' As the words passed from her lips, a laser beam ripped through the barrel she was crouched behind, and a torrent of purple sludge sprayed all down her front.

'Remember,' said Digger. 'Have faith in yourself and anything is possible.'

But Max wasn't listening. He was completely and utterly frozen with fear, the demands that the others had placed on him finally 'crushing' him under their weight. His heart was beating so fast that he thought it was going to explode, and his stomach churned like Stevie's after eating ten hot dogs.

Young Master.

M.U.M's voice cut through the wave of nausea that was washing over him and brought Max to his senses.

M.U.M, where have you been?

Apologies, young master... I was forced to attend to some unwelcome visitors.

Unwelcome visitors?

Two guards were attempting to access the ship's hull with a welding torch. Let us just say that I gave them an electrifying welcome.

Was that a joke? I thought computers didn't do that?

We do not, but I sensed that your mood needed lightening. How can I assist you?

Another laser beam whizzed over the group's

heads and exploded against the wall behind them, showering the air with clumps of molten metal.

I can't do this, M.U.M. Everyone expects me to be this big hero, but I'm not that person. I'm Max, good at video games, but not much else.

These video games, they allow the character that you play to receive enhancements to their abilities, do they not?

You mean like upgrades, power-ups, things like that?

Correct.

Yeah, what about them?

What if I were to upgrade you?

Upgrade me? What do you mean?

Perhaps it would be easier if I showed you.

Max felt a sudden surge of electricity flow through his body, and his vision began to blur as an intense white light seemed to burn itself into the back of his retinas. Instinctively, he rubbed his eyes, blinking several times in an attempt to clear them. Then, as quickly as it had appeared, it was gone, and it soon became clear that something extraordinary had happened.

Max no longer saw the world in the 'normal'

sense. Everything, and everyone, had become pixelated, as if he'd just put on his virtual reality headset and stepped inside a video game.

How are you doing this? asked Max in amazement.

The link that we share, it has enabled me to tap directly into your nervous system. I have temporarily enhanced both your physical and mental capabilities. How do you feel?

I feel... I feel... great, actually.

In fact, Max had never felt better. His whole body tingled, and he could feel raw energy pulsing through his veins. The dangers that he faced were still very real, but his confidence had soared. By viewing his environment as if it were a video game, the pressures that had threatened to consume him had melted away. This was a world that he knew and felt comfortable in; a world in which he no longer had to zip up the fur-lined hood of his anorak tightly around his face. Most importantly though, it was one in which he excelled. Max didn't need a controller in his hand anymore—he *was* the controller.

'Max! What's wrong?' Stevie's pixelated, neon framed, face came looming into view.

'Nothing, Stevie,' replied Max. 'I'm fine.'

'Thought we'd lost you there for a second, Pipsqueak,' said Lucinda. Another laser beam shot in her direction, and another barrel of purple sludge exploded all over her. 'Oh, this is getting ridiculous now!' she exclaimed, parting her ooze matted hair.

'No one will blame you if you cannot go through with this,' said Digger. 'It is a lot to ask of you, young one.'

'It's OK,' replied Max. 'I can do this.' Taking a deep breath, he stood up to his full height. Even on tiptoes, the barrels towered over his diminutive frame, and he struggled to see over them. There was only one thing for it; he would have to step out from behind their protection.

Sure enough, a laser beam shot instantly in his direction. However, Max saw it coming and coolly sidestepped out the way. He'd always had quick reflexes; it's what made him such a good gamer. But now, with M.U.M's help, they had become even quicker. In fact, his whole body felt tense, primed and ready for action. What exactly *had* M.U.M done to him? It was time to find out.

As he raised the ray gun to fire, a pair of glowing green targeting sights appeared before his very eyes. Somehow, the crosshairs were being projected directly on to his eyeballs themselves, and they had just locked on to the guard stooped behind the wooden crates.

Max fired. *ZAP!* Surprisingly, it wasn't a laser beam that shot out. It was more like a lightning bolt, which seared through the air in jagged silver fingers, hitting the crates in an explosion of wooden splinters.

'Ouchy, ouchy, ouchy!' cried out the guard, holding his splinter-riddled bottom in his hands as he fled from the room.

Max ducked back down behind the barrels and looked closely at the ray gun. The lightning bolt had been unexpected, and now he saw the reason why. On top of it was a small round dial with four different options engraved around it: *Laser Beam, Lightning Bolt, Miniaturisation Ray* and *Wormhole.* He thought for a second and then turned the dial to *Miniaturization Ray.* It was time to deal with the guard to his right.

ZAP! A sparkling red beam of light shone from the muzzle of the ray gun and fell like a spotlight onto the stack of barrels. Immediately, they shrank down to the size of thimbles, exposing the guard that had been crouched behind them. *ZAP!* Before the guard had a chance to react, a second ray enveloped his body in a bright red glow, and he quickly reduced in size until he was no bigger than one of Max's toy figures.

'Snot, ATTACK!' commanded Stevie.

The guard let out a high-pitched shriek of terror as Snot, who was now at least twice his size, chased him out the room.

That just left Grimhorn who, up until now, had remained motionless the whole time, still under the impression that he was somehow invisible.

'AATCHOO!' The inevitable happened, and Grimhorn let out an immense sneeze that shook his whole body. Convinced he'd just broken his cover, he attempted to delicately tiptoe towards the door, which when you weigh more than a pickup truck is easier said than done.

Max turned the dial on the ray gun to *Wormhole.* He was unsure what it meant, but it sounded less drastic than the other options. After all, he did have a bit of a soft spot for the nitwitted numbskull.

ZAP! The very air itself appeared to rip apart, and a whirling, roaring spiral of colours, like a tornado that had been flipped on its side, opened up next to Grimhorn. Despite his huge size, it easily sucked him in, tossing him around as if he were in a washing machine on a spin cycle.

'Nice knowings you!' called out Grimhorn. He let out one final sneeze and then was gone, the wormhole collapsing in on itself before disappearing completely with a *POP!*

'You know, I'll actually miss the big guy,' said Stevie. 'I can't put my finger on it, but there was something strangely familiar about the great, smelly ol' snot bag.'

'Yeah, can't for the life of me think what it might be,' said Lucinda, rolling her eyes.

'What will happen to him?' asked Max. Now that the group was out of immediate danger, his vision had returned to normal, and he felt the muscles in his body relax as the surge of energy that had flowed through them gradually began to subside.

'Passing through a wormhole is like walking through a door without knowing what is on the other side,' explained Digger. 'He could just as easily reappear in the next room as he could on a planet at the distant edge of this universe. There really is no way of telling.'

'So, he'll be OK?'

'In theory, yes. You did well, young one. I am impressed.'

Max gave a coy shrug of his shoulders. 'Thanks. By the way, I'm back in contact with M.U.M. The map shows a turbo lift not too far from here. It'll take us straight to the docking bay.'

'Then show us the way, young one.'

As the group made their way out the room, Max allowed himself a small smile. He'd decided not to let the others into his amazing secret—not just yet.

CHAPTER THIRTEEN

A DEADLY GUFF

On an ice moon several million miles away, a swirling vortex of colours opened in the snow-filled sky. After several seconds, it spat out Grimhorn, who plummeted into a large snowdrift. *PAARRRPPPP!* Fortunately, for Grimhorn at least, his dinosaur-sized bottom burp blew a hole in the snow, ejecting a puff of snowflakes high into the air. After much scrabbling about under the surface, his head finally appeared from out of it.

'What happen to Grimhorn?' he said, the snow falling away as he slowly heaved himself to his feet. 'Oh, me remembers now. Swirly, whirly thing gobble Grimhorn up. But where is me now?' His voice, which was normally muffled by his snot filled sinuses, was unusually clear and distinct. 'Grimhorn feel good for change. Me not even sneezing.' His huge chest expanded as he took in a deep breath of the crisp, cool air.

All around him was an uninterrupted blanket of white snow. No trees, no bushes and most importantly of all—no mould spores to make him sneeze. It was also ice cold, far too cold for normal dinosaurs, but then Grimhorn was anything but.

As he continued to take in his surroundings, Grimhorn noticed several trails of disturbed snow, as if something underneath it was burrowing its way towards him. Before his miniscule brain had the chance to work out what it might be, dozens of small bear-like creatures suddenly emerged and shook the snow from their furry heads.

Grimhorn looked down at the tiny creatures and decided to introduce himself, thrusting a giant hand towards them in greeting. 'Me Grimhorn. Pleased to be meeting you.'

At the sound of his voice, all the creatures fell to their knees and began to chant, worshipping Grimhorn as if he were a god who'd fallen from the sky.

'Um... No needs to be scared, me not hurt you.'

One of the creatures scurried up to him and, holding a large cube of yellow snow above its head, reverentially offered it up to him.

'Lemon slushy?' asked Grimhorn. 'For me? Ta very much.' He bent down and gently clasped the cube between his fingers, dropping it into his gaping mouth. 'Mmmm! Grimhorn like. You got more?'

The creatures let out a happy chirping sound and disappeared back under the snow. Just as he began to wonder if he'd offended them, Grimhorn felt a tremor beneath his feet, and he toppled back with a *THUD!* onto his bottom. More tremors followed, and he began to slowly rise as a multitude of small furry paws hoisted him onto their shoulders.

'Hmm... No sneezing and no mean ol' boss to order me around. Methinks me going to like it here.'

And with that, the creatures carried Grimhorn off to his new, sneeze-free life, and as much 'lemon slushy' as he could ever hope to eat.

The four salivating Velociraptors strained at the ends of a heavy iron-link chain, pulling a stumbling, bumbling guard along behind them. Like bloodhounds, their pointy little snouts sniffed feverishly at the floor, desperate for the scent of the escaped prisoners. Suddenly, one of them stopped dead in its tracks, its nostrils flaring and twitching. Pausing briefly, it peeled back its lips to reveal a cruel smile of needle-sharp teeth.

The hunt was on.

Take a right, young master.

A long metal walkway stretched out in front of the group, sheer drops into darkness either side of it. At the other end, vaguely discernible in the distance, was the turbo lift that would deliver them to the docking bay. Freedom was within their grasp.

Max cautiously led the group forward, his eyes darting back and forth as he scanned the walkway for any signs of movement. In the background, over the wail of the ship's alarm, he could hear the thump of huge dinosaur

feet running around aimlessly, and confused
mutterings echoed along the corridors.

*M.U.M, I've not mentioned it to the others, but
I'm worried.*

What is concerning you, young master?

*Even if we do make it back to the ship, what
chance do we have of escape? You said it before;
nothing can outrun a Crocodile class destroyer.*

*Do not worry; it is all in hand. I took the liberty
of uploading a virus into the destroyer's computer.
When I transmit a signal, it will automatically
disable the ship's engines and make a pursuit
impossible.*

Looks like you've thought of everything.

*There is more. ED-21 has almost finished repairs
to the Multiverse Drive. By the time you are back on
board, it will be possible to make the jump to another
universe.*

*Wow, you really have been busy. I guess it's over
to me then.*

The group had covered almost half the length
of the walkway, when Max felt the hairs on
the back of his neck rise, and the same surge
of energy that he'd felt before rushed through
his body. Whirling around, his eyes zoomed in

like the telescopic sight of a sniper's rifle on the pixelated guard stood at the other end.

But the guard was the least of his worries.

'Velociraptors!' shouted Max. 'Move!'

The four Velociraptors were incredibly quick, even with Max's newly improved reflexes, and by the time he'd raised the ray gun to fire, they were almost upon him.

ZAP! The lead Velociraptor was encompassed by the red glow of the miniaturisation ray and immediately started to shrink. Its viciousness though, remained undiminished, and it proceeded to enthusiastically savage the bottom of Max's trousers.

He flicked it off with a shake of his leg and clicked the ray gun to *Lightning Bolt* as a second Velociraptor leapt into the air, its claws aimed directly at his throat. Instinctively, Max ducked, and he saw the look of triumph in the Velociraptor's eyes quickly turn to terror as it sailed over the edge of the walkway and down into the sea of darkness below.

'Max, help!' cried out Stevie.

Whilst Max had been busy trying to defend them, the rest of the group had fled in the direction of the turbo lift. Unfortunately, their route was now blocked by a third Velociraptor that had sprung over their heads and was now stood snarling in front of them.

'I'm afraid I've got my own problems!' shouted back Max.

Unlike its brothers, the fourth Velociraptor had held back and was stealthily making its way towards him. *ZAP!* It jumped out the way of the lightning bolt, a charred, smoking hole in place of where it had previously stood. This one was going to be tricky.

'Get behind me,' said Digger. Using his body as a shield, he put himself between the advancing Velociraptor and the children. 'Be brave, younglings. Our deaths will be quick.'

Paarrrpppppp! Stevie let off a very long, very high-pitched, Tommy Squeaker of a fart.

'Oh great,' said Lucinda. 'Here I am, facing certain death, and the last thing I'm going to hear is the sound of Gassy Gut's bowels erupting.'

'Sorry,' said Stevie. 'I always get like this when I'm nervous. But, better out…'

'*Than in.* Yeah, yeah, we know,' said Lucinda, shaking her head.

However, Stevie's stinky flatulence had a rather unexpected effect. Just when it looked like the Velociraptor was about to pounce, it let out a pitiful screech and promptly keeled over, dead.

'What's going on?' asked Stevie, looking more than a little confused.

Digger gave a throaty chuckle. 'Velociraptors have an acute sense of smell. It would appear that the intestinal gases of your species are deadly to them.'

'No, just Stevie's,' said Lucinda, laughing nervously. 'I always said you did killer farts.'

'Er, guys, a little help...?' called out Max, who was still busy fending off the one remaining Velociraptor. If it was able to avoid laser beams and lightning bolts, how would it fare against a wormhole?

ZAP! The air in front of Max tore open, and the spinning disc of colours easily sucked in the Velociraptor, which disappeared with little more than a whimper.

But there was now a new problem. The wormhole had opened up right next to Max, and its raging winds were threatening to suck him in as well.

'GUYS!' exclaimed Max, this time more urgently as his feet began to lift off the floor. He thought back to all the times he'd seen his mum suck up spiders with the vacuum cleaner, and now he knew exactly how they felt.

Digger and Lucinda grabbed on to Max's left leg, whilst Stevie anchored his right. Even Snot tried to help by hanging off the seat of Max's trousers by his mouth. Try as they might though, one by one they began to lift slowly off the floor.

'It's no good,' shouted Max over the roar of the swirling vortex. 'Let go of me or we'll all get sucked in.'

'Not so fast, Pipsqueak,' shouted back Lucinda. 'You got us into this mess, so you're going to get us out of it. Whether you like it or not—you're stuck with us.'

The wormhole gave one final tug and then seemed to give up, coughing and sputtering like an old car engine. Finally, it imploded with a *POP!* and sent the group crashing to the floor.

'I'm going to wake up in a minute and realise this was all a bad dream,' said Lucinda, who was lying spreadeagled on her back. She screwed her eyes tightly shut, paused, and then opened them again. Perched on her chest, his big bug eyes staring down inquisitively at her, was Snot. Lucinda let out a long sigh. 'OK, so not a dream then. Now, GET OFF ME YOU SLIMY, TOAD-FACED GARGOYLE!'

Dusting themselves down, the group resumed their journey towards the turbo lift.

'Hold on a minute,' said Stevie. 'What about the guard?'

Max chuckled. 'He's a bit tied up at the moment.'

In the background, the guard was roaring in pain, desperately grabbing at his bottom as the miniaturized Velociraptor happily swung from his tail by its snapping little jaws.

'Looks like we're home free,' said Lucinda as the turbo lift doors slid apart.

'Let's not get carried away,' said Max. 'One step at a time.'

He was worried that his vision hadn't returned to normal. Clearly, they weren't out of danger yet.

CHAPTER FOURTEEN

THE TRAP

The turbo lift doors opened to reveal the docking
bay, a vast, brightly lit area, populated by a
variety of small attack craft. Towering above
them all though, like a great, ugly carbuncle, was
the *Cosmo II*.

'I never thought I'd say this,' said Lucinda, 'but
I'm actually glad to see the big rust bucket.'

A small mountain of snoring guards were piled
up next to it, casualties of M.U.M's *electrifying*
welcome.

'Careful,' said Max, beckoning the others to
follow. 'Something's not right.'

The neon glow of his pixelated surroundings
had started to throb, as if alerting him to an
unseen presence. It was quiet, too quiet, and
the only sound that could be heard was the
low hum of the destroyer's hyperdrive as it

continued on its relentless course towards Terra Prime.

'What are you on about?' asked Lucinda, brushing Max aside. 'I knew it couldn't last. You're being a Nervous Nellie again.'

'No, Lucinda—WAIT!'

But it was too late. A red glow surrounded Lucinda's body, and she immediately began to shrink down in size until she was no bigger than a doll's house figurine.

'I've really got to learn to keep my big mouth shut,' squeaked Lucinda, as laser beams, every colour of the rainbow, erupted all around her.

'It's a trap!' shouted Max. 'Get down!'

Scooping up Lucinda, he ushered the others under the protective wing of one of the attack craft. Where were the laser blasts coming from? He felt the muscles behind his eyeballs tighten as his new telescopic vision adjusted focus. Zooming in and out, they scanned the room for danger. Nothing.

'I can't see any guards,' yelled Max, showers of sparks erupting all around him. 'There's too many ships in the way.'

'Neither can I...' replied Digger, his nose twitching, 'but I can definitely smell them!'

Maybe this will help, young master.

The array of small ships seemed to shimmer until only their outline was visible. Somehow, Max was able to see straight through them, as clearly as if he were looking through a window.

X-Ray vision? enquired Max. *Any other surprises you want to let me in on, M.U.M?*

Then they would not be surprises, young master.

Max chuckled. There was no arguing with M.U.M's logic. With his new upgrade, he was able to see a small army of guards 'hidden' around the room. Even though the *Cosmo II* was only a stone's throw away, it would be impossible to lead the others safely to it without being cut down by a hail of laser blasts.

There's too many guards, M.U.M. I might be able to stop a couple of them, but I'm not fast enough to handle the rest on my own.

In that case, maybe another surprise is in order.

To his astonishment, Max felt a fresh rush of energy surge through his body. Adrenaline began to flood his bloodstream, and his heart pulsated like the revving engine of a sports car waiting for the lights to turn green.

'Look after her,' said Max, gently handing

Lucinda to Stevie.

'You can't leave me with *him*, Pipsqueak,' cried Lucinda, squirming between Stevie's big sausage fingers.

'Hey, who you calling Pipsqueak—pipsqueak!' replied Max with a smile.

Lucinda's high-pitched objections were quickly silenced by Stevie, who dropped her into the murky depths of his coat pocket.

'What do you intend to do, young one?' asked Digger gravely.

'Get the others safely to the ship,' said Max. 'Let me take care of the guards.'

'But young one, we are outnumbered. You will be killed.'

'Don't worry about me; I've got a couple of tricks up my sleeve. Now go. I'll provide a distraction.'

GREEN! Max roared off the starting line, his feet barely touching the floor as he launched himself through the air. A fresh volley of laser beams fired in his direction, but he was too quick for them, and they passed through empty space, where he'd been just milliseconds before.

'Over here!' taunted Max, his body a blur of movement. 'No, here—TOO SLOW!'

Several of the guards made a clumsy grab for him, but they ended up with nothing more than handfuls of thin air as he slipped elusively through their fingers.

'Hey, not fair!' complained one of the guards. 'You not play nice!'

Max had a plan. Furtively, he was drawing the guards out into the open, gathering them together like a sheepdog herds up sheep. 'Hey, slow coach!' he called out, as the last stray guard lumbered into position. The Terrasaurs weren't the only ones who could set a trap.

On the wall, tightly wound in a reel, was a fire hose. Max grabbed the nozzle and literally ran rings around the guards, the hose snaking around them until they were all bound together in one groaning, confused bundle.

'Max! Get on board!' shouted Stevie from the ramp of the *Cosmo II*. In all the chaos, Digger had managed to lead the others safely to the ship.

Max was about to react, when a torrent of Velociraptors poured into the docking bay and formed a snarling, hissing circle around him.

'Stevie! GO!' shouted Max. His breathing had become laboured, and he was gasping for breath.

M.U.M, there's something wrong. I can barely breathe.

You have temporarily exhausted your body's supply of adrenalin, young master. I cannot enhance what you no longer possess. According to my sensors, you are about to lose consciousness.

Max's limbs felt like lead, and the ray gun fell with a clatter from his limp hand onto the floor. The room began to spin, and he looked on helplessly as the ring of Velociraptors slowly began to tighten around him, their mouths salivating at the prospect of the meal to come.

'Max, above you!' shouted Stevie. He'd ignored Max's instruction to go and had somehow managed to clamber into the open cockpit of one of the attack craft.

Struggling to stay on his feet, Max tilted back his head. His vision had begun to blur, but he could just make out a strip light hanging from the ceiling high above him.

'JUMP!' urged Stevie. 'JUMP!' He was desperately jabbing his fingers at the ship's controls, seemingly in an attempt to find something.

And then, he did.

The ship's laser cannons sprang into life, their motion sensors locking on to the nearest moving thing. With a thunderous blast, they fired two purple bolts of pure energy, and Max and the Velociraptors disappeared in a huge billowing fireball that rose in a mushroom shape into the air.

As the smoke began to clear, it revealed a deep circular crater seared into the docking bay floor, flames still licking at its edge. Everything had been vapourised, and nothing but small piles of ash remained.

'Max! *NOOOOOO!*' With tears in his eyes, Stevie jumped down into the crater, scrabbling around on his hands and knees as he vainly searched for any signs of life. There were none.

A tear slowly trickled down Stevie's cheek. 'I'm sorry, Max. I've let you down again.'

'Stevie, up here,' came a faint voice from above.

Barely visible through the cloud of smoke, Max was clung sloth-like from the strip light. Somehow, at the very last second, he'd managed to jump clear of the blast, rocketing above the fireball in a truly superhuman effort.

'Max! You're alive!' exclaimed Stevie.

'Catch,' whispered Max.

'What?' asked Stevie.

'Catch.'

Max fell like a stone into Stevie's outstretched arms. His vision had returned to normal, but a tunnel of darkness appeared to be closing in around him.

'You did it,' said Stevie, cradling his friend's limp body.

'No, Stevie. *We* did it.'

And with that, the darkness consumed Max completely.

CHAPTER FIFTEEN

A NEW BEGINNING

'*WHAAAAT?*'

Admiral Tyrannus stomped onto the bridge of his ship, clearly in an agitated mood. He would have been terrifying, but for the fact he was wearing a bright pink onesie and had a melting white mask of moisturising cream dripping down his face in big unctuous blobs.

'You mean to tell me the Earth boy's no longer on board the ship?'

'Er, yeah, boss. Sorry, boss,' said a guard, trying to stifle a snigger.

'So, go after them—IDIOT!'

'Er, yeah, about that, boss. There's a slight problem.'

Admiral Tyrannus scrutinized the guard's face. '*Problem?* What kind of problem?'

The guard hesitated. 'Um, well, er...'

'Get on with it will you. If I leave this face cream on for too long it brings me out in a terrible rash.'

'The, er, boy did something to the ship, boss.'

'Then fix it. It's not as if they've somehow managed to disable our ships' engines and therefore make any attempt to pursue them impossible… *is it?*'

'Funny you should say that, boss…'

Admiral Tyrannus slumped his head forward, as if all the air in his body had been sucked out, and closed his eyes. 'Do you mean to tell me that every ship in the mighty Terrasaurian fleet has been crippled by a scrawny child and his ragtag bunch of misfits?'

'Pretty much, boss. It's some kind of computer virus.'

The Admiral's eyes shot open. 'Computer virus? Well, why didn't you say? How hard can this *electrickery* nonsense be?' He pushed the guard out of the way and sat hunched over a control console, wiggling his ridiculously small fingers like a pianist about to perform a concerto. 'Now, let's see what we're up against.'

With his tongue lolling out of his mouth

in concentration, Admiral Tyrannus began clumsily crashing his hands down upon a keyboard, and a series of strange green symbols slowly started to fill a computer screen. Every now and again he would pause, angrily mutter something under his breath, and then resume once more. Eventually, after a very, *very* long time, a computerised voice boomed out from a speaker.

'ENGINES BACK ONLINE.'

'Ha!' exclaimed Admiral Tyrannus smugly. 'What did I tell you? I've got brains as well as beauty!'

But his arrogance was short-lived.

'SELF DESTRUCT SEQUENCE INITIATED,' continued the booming voice. 'SHIP WILL SELF DESTRUCT IN 5... 4... 3... 2...1...'

The Admiral's jaw dropped. 'Oh, *poop!*'

Like a dying star going supanova, the shockwave from the exploding destroyer travelled far and wide. When it eventually caught up with the *Cosmo II,* it had lost most of its energy, merely buffeting the ship as if it were a fishing boat on a mildly stormy sea.

'What was that?' asked Max, as he struggled to sit up in bed. His head was throbbing with the worst headache ever.

'Probably just another meteor shower,' replied Stevie, who'd been keeping a bedside vigil. He produced a can of Glurg Cola from out of a pocket and handed it to Max. 'Doctor's orders. M.U.M says you need to top up your energy levels.'

Max smiled and reached for the bowl of fruit next to him. 'Thanks, but I'm not so sure that's what she had in mind.'

'Suit yourself,' said Stevie, pulling back the ring pull and taking a large swig from the can.

'How did you know?' asked Max, methodically peeling back a banana skin.

'Know what?'

'That I'd be able to jump that high, you know, back in the docking bay.'

Stevie chuckled. 'No offence, but we've both dodged more than our fair share of P.E lessons. There's no way you were pulling off those acrobatic moves on your own.'

'Thanks! But no, you're right, M.U.M may have had *something* to do with it,' said Max, a twinkle in his eye.

He was about to offer further explanation when ED-21 came rolling into the room, a stethoscope placed neatly around his neck. He was accompanied by Digger who, with a hearty meal inside him and a change of clothes, looked years younger than when the children had first encountered him back in the cell.

'Ah, good to have you back in the land of the living, young one. You had us worried for a moment.'

As ED-21 fussed around him, Max listened to the others as they recounted the events after he'd passed out. Apparently, Stevie had carried him back on board the *Cosmo II*, and Digger had then used the laser drill to blast open the destroyer's docking bay doors, smashing their way to freedom through the smoking remains. The Terrasaurs had attempted to follow, but M.U.M had sent the signal disabling their ships' engines.

'And what about Lucinda?' asked Max. 'Is she OK?'

'Lucinda!' exclaimed Stevie. 'I'd forgotten all about her!' He thrust his hand deep inside his coat pocket and, after a second or two of rummaging around, pulled out a very dishevelled looking Lucinda.

'Idiot!' she squeaked. 'I could hardly breathe in there!' She was covered from head to toe in a mixture of melted chocolate and crisp crumbs, looking very much like something you might buy in an after school cake sale.

'Yeah, sorry about that,' said Stevie sheepishly. 'But at least you were safe.' Carefully, he lowered Lucinda down onto Max's bed covers, their creased ridges forming a mountainous landscape around her.

'Safe! Have you seen what's inside your pockets? I'm lucky to be alive!'

'Fine!' said Stevie. 'Next time, I won't bother!'

'Now, now, younglings. Calm down,' said Digger, crouching down to address Lucinda. 'The effects of the miniaturisation ray are only temporary, young one. You will return to your normal size... eventually.'

'I should hope so,' said Lucinda. 'Before I drown in this thing's drool.' Snot had jumped up onto Max's bed and was sat wheezing affectionately beside her.

'Thank goodness we've got you to keep the peace, Digger,' said Max. 'I don't know what we'd do without you.'

'Ah, yes, about that,' said Digger hesitantly. 'I am afraid the time has come for us to go our separate ways.'

'What?' asked Max, clearly surprised. 'You can't leave us now. We need you too much.'

'As do my people, young one. Thanks to you, the Terrasaurs are in retreat. But this universe is my home, and it needs my help to rebuild it.'

'But, we'll be lost without you. *I'll* be lost without you.'

'Your path may not be clear, young one, but it is a path nonetheless. You do not need me to show you the way. Do you remember what I said to you before? Have faith in yourself...'

'*And anything is possible,*' finished Max. 'Yes, I remember.'

'And see how far you have come in such a short time.'

Max thought back to the shy, awkward boy he'd left behind on the school bus. 'You're right,' he said. 'I'm sorry. I was being selfish.'

'Do not be so harsh on yourself, young one. Besides, you do not need me when you have such good friends to help you.'

'What, even Lucinda?' interrupted Stevie, screwing up his face.

'Yes, even Lucinda,' replied Digger with a wry smile. 'She may be rude, irritating, obnoxious and arrogant, but she is not all bad.'

Lucinda called up from the bed. 'Er, guys? I know I might look like something from *Toy Story*, but I can still hear you know.'

'Attention,' said M.U.M. 'We are being hailed by a Moleian ship. It wishes to know our intentions.'

Max paused for a second. 'Tell them we've one passenger for pick up.' He threw back his bedcovers and jumped out of bed, sending Lucinda flying through the air. 'Come on you lot—we've got work to do.'

'You know, I think I preferred the old Pipsqueak,' muttered Lucinda as Stevie picked her up. 'He never used to be this bossy.'

'I heard that,' called back Max. 'Now hurry up, or I'll have Stevie feed you to Snot.'

Lucinda gulped loudly, her little face staring up at Stevie. 'He wouldn't? *You* wouldn't?'

'I wouldn't, but Max, I'm not so sure these days,' said Stevie, trying to keep a straight face.

'Then what are we waiting for?' asked Lucinda. 'You heard him—hurry up!'

Digger's face stared back from the control room's viewscreen. 'Farewell for now my friends. Our paths shall cross again.'

The viewscreen shimmered, and Max watched in silence as the small Moleian ship hurriedly sped into the distance.

'Well, I guess that's level one completed,' he said, turning to the others.

Stevie chuckled and put his arm around Max. 'Yeah, but I get the feeling level two's going to be *a lot* harder.'

'Well, there's only one way to find out,' said Lucinda, who was perched on Stevie's shoulder like a particularly annoying parrot.

Max sat down in the captain's chair. It was still far too big for him, and yet it somehow felt more comfortable than before. 'ED-21, would you do the honours?'

'Of course, sir. I would be happy to...'

'NOOOOOO!' shouted all three children, bursting into laughter.

'I do not understand, sir,' said ED-21. 'Do you wish me to activate the Multiverse Drive, or not?'

'Never mind,' said Max grinning. 'Probably best I do it.' He turned to Stevie. 'Ready?'

'Ready,' replied Stevie, strapping himself into his chair. Snot jumped up and promptly fell asleep in a snoring heap on his lap.

'Hey! What about me?' said Lucinda.

'You're right,' said Max. 'Best secure Lucinda, Stevie.'

'*Secure?*' asked Lucinda suspiciously. 'Oh no— not again! You dare...'

'All secured,' declared Stevie, smirking and gently patting his coat pocket.

'Right then,' said Max, his finger hovering over a big red button. 'Let's go find my dad!'

'Multiverse Drive engaged. Prepare for Quantum jump.'

EPILOGUE
I SPY

Like a plastic straw sucking up the remnants of a particularly thick milkshake, the vile green liquid made a revolting slurping sound as it travelled slowly up and around the transparent tube.

'Agent 84, report,' said the Overlord. His voice was hoarse and rasping.

A tall figure dressed all in black stepped forward. In the dull lighting of the throne room, you could be forgiven for thinking he was human. But look again, and you might notice the fine, almost indistinguishable, hinge running down one side of his face, allowing it to be flipped open and access gained to the circuitry inside. Agent 84 was an android.

'It has been done, sire,' replied Agent 84. His voice, like his face, had been designed to replicate a human's but had a telltale electronic edge to it.

'A trans-dimensional tracking device was attached to the boy's ship before he made the jump.'

'Good, I knew that fool Tyrannus would fail me. Still, I think you'll agree, he makes a rather attractive addition to my collection.'

Using his skeletal hand, the Overlord flicked a switch on his throne's armrest, and a spotlight immediately illuminated Admiral Tyrannus. Well, what was left of him. A ghastly, rictus grin had been stitched across his face, and his body resembled an overly stuffed sausage skin, wisps of smoke still drifting from the charred remains of his pink onesie. He was surrounded by an army of similar 'statues'—creatures from across the Multiverse that had failed to do the Overlord's bidding.

'He appears to be missing a hand, sire,' said Agent 84. 'Was it lost in the explosion?'

'Let me tell you something about a Tyrannosaurus Rex's hand, Agent 84,' said the Overlord. 'It is far too small, in comparison to its huge size, to serve any useful purpose. However, it fits *me* like a glove.' He raised the newly attached clawed hand to his hooded face. 'Call it a souvenir of my time spent here.'

He began to laugh, wheezing and coughing unpleasantly as he did so. A tube under his cloak shuddered, and another gob of green gunk flew up it and disappeared into his throne.

'Very good, sire.'

'Yes, I thought so. But enough fun…'

The Overlord's voice took on an even more sinister tone than usual, and his eyes glowed a fiery red amidst the blackness of his cowl.

'BRING ME THE BOY!' he raged, slamming down his fists. 'BRING ME MAX VOLTAGE!'

TO BE CONTINUED…

MAX VOLTAGE WILL RETURN IN

MAX VOLTAGE: PLANET TERROR

Dear reader,

I hope you enjoyed reading Max Voltage: Multiverse Mayhem, the first book in the Max Voltage series. If you'd like to find out when book two is due for release, then be sure to get an adult to check out jameslovesmglit.wordpress.com or alternatively they can follow me on Twitter @JamesLovesMGLit for all the latest updates.

What universe will Max and his friends jump to next?

Will Agent 84 succeed in tracking them down?

Or will Planet Terror destroy them all?
... And will Stevie *ever* stop farting?!

For the answers to these, and many other questions, be sure to keep your peepers peeled for book two in the series:

MAX VOLTAGE: PLANET TERROR

Until next time…

James Love

Printed in Poland
by Amazon Fulfillment
Poland Sp. z o.o., Wrocław